Magnetic Fields
An Amish Love Story

by
R. P. Gabriel

1663 LIBERTY DRIVE, SUITE 200
BLOOMINGTON, INDIANA 47403
(800) 839-8640
WWW.AUTHORHOUSE.COM

AuthorHouse™
1663 Liberty Drive, Suite 200
Bloomington, IN 47403
www.authorhouse.com
Phone: 1-800-839-8640

AuthorHouse™ *UK Ltd.*
500 Avebury Boulevard
Central Milton Keynes, MK9 2BE
www.authorhouse.co.uk
Phone: 08001974150

© 2007 R. P. Gabriel. All rights reserved.

No part of this book may be reproduced, stored in a retrieval system, or transmitted by any means without the written permission of the author.

First published by AuthorHouse 9/20/2007

ISBN: 1-4259-1058-0 (sc)
ISBN: 1-4259-1059-9 (hc)

Library of Congress Control Number: 2005911245

Printed in the United States of America
Bloomington, Indiana

This book is printed on acid-free paper.

I wish to dedicate this book to my wife and four children.

ACKNOWLEDGEMENTS

I want to thank my daughter. Without her inspiration, this novella would never have been conceived, let alone written.

I also want to thank my wife. Her musicianship and constructive advice greatly helped to keep this story grounded in reality.

CHAPTER I

From the bedroom window, the Pennsylvania farmland is a sight to behold.

The early morning sunlight splashes over the checkerboard farms, which undulate from the flatlands onto the rolling hills like a living quilt, reaching all the way to the horizon.

The light chases an early autumn breeze through an open window and into the bedroom.

The room is stark. A kerosene lamp sits on a nightstand next to the bed. Worn, black work boots lie next to a closet. Inside the small closet, a pair of black pants and several white, short-sleeved shirts hang neatly on wire hangers.

A young man, age twenty-two, sits on a bare, hardwood floor with his back up against the wooden frame of his bed. His genetic heritage may explain his apparent indifference to the coldness of his bedroom.

He looks intently through the window for a moment, and then looks down, then up, then down; his eyes moving in and out of the light. In his fingers, a small paint brush is dancing on a small canvas. The canvas is leaning up against the legs of a straight-backed wooden chair. His brushstrokes are precise and sure as he recreates, on the canvas, the landscape seen in the distance beyond his window.

A knock on his door startles him. He jumps up, walks over to the door, and opens it. A tall, gray-haired man with a full-length beard stands at the doorway.

"I wanted to make sure that you were awake, Jonathan," his father, Paul, says.

Jonathan's father, like himself, is tall and lean, with hard muscles and chiseled, symmetrical features. The physical differences between them are what one might expect, considering their twenty-five-year age difference. The father wears a beard with no mustache.

Upon marriage, Amish men are obligated to grow out their beards. And although beards are mandatory for married men, mustaches are strictly forbidden. The rationale for this rather odd rule is that, from their earliest origins in Europe in the 1600s, the Amish have associated mustaches with soldiers, and therefore, the military. And because they are strict pacifists, the Amish shun military service, which they associate with violence, or the potential for violence; and so the early Amish did not want their men resembling soldiers in any way. Therefore, a policy of no mustaches in married men was established more than three centuries ago, and still holds strong to this day.

Jonathan's father speaks with a subtle German accent, as do most members of his generation. Jonathan speaks less formally, and with no German accent.

"Dad, I'll be right down," Jonathan replies. "I just have to get my boots on."

"I will see you in the kitchen, son. We have much work to do today."

"Yes, father, just like every day."

"Yes, son, just like every day. But it is this work which keeps us strong. It is the glue that binds our family and our people."

"Oh really? I thought it was the cow dung and the pig slobber that glued us together," Jonathan mutters to himself.

Paul stops and turns around. "I'm sorry, son. I didn't hear what you said."

"It was nothing, Dad. I'll see you in the kitchen."

Jonathan sits down on the wooden chair and slowly begins

putting on his boots. The long day has only just begun, and he already looks tired. When he finishes lacing up his boots, he gets up and walks over to the closet. He removes a wide-brimmed straw hat from a hook in the closet, takes a deep breath, and slowly walks out of the bedroom.

The Schaeffer family members are sitting around the kitchen table and eating as if they have not had a morsel of food for days. Jonathan's mother, Elizabeth, is standing at the kitchen counter, slicing a loaf of homemade bread, still warm from the oven.

His father looks up from his plate.

Jonathan walks over to the table and takes a couple of thick slices of still-warm bread off the large serving dish. With a large spoon, he places a mound of scrambled eggs on top of one slice of bread, and then slaps another slice of bread on top of that.

He takes a big bite from the egg sandwich while walking towards the back door.

He stops at the door. "I'll see you guys out at the barn," he says over his shoulder, just before opening and walking out the door.

"That's not enough … food," Paul utters, just before the screen door slams shut. He puts his fork down, and through the kitchen window, he watches Jonathan walking towards the barn. He then looks over at Elizabeth, who is also watching their oldest son.

Paul looks at the plates of the other children sitting at the table. "You kids seem quite finished. Let's get about our chores, children. We have much work to do today."

The two younger boys scramble out of their chairs and scurry out to the barn to join their older brother, Jonathan. Their sister, Mary, age seventeen, hurries outside to start the day's laundry chores. Two-year-old Rebecca remains in her high chair, busily adding to her mess on the floor.

After the screen door closes behind Mary, Elizabeth turns to Paul. "I know what you're thinking, but not everyone is cut out for the farm life, Paul."

Paul starts buttering a slice of bread. "That is not what I am worried about, Beth," he replies calmly.

"You're speaking about baptism again, then, aren't you?"

"Yes, I am."

"It must be his decision about baptism, and no one else's. That is our way. He should make his choice only when he's ready," she says, her tone firm.

"The church elders are becoming impatient with his indecisiveness, and so am I."

"Again, it is his life. Not theirs, and not yours, Paul," Elizabeth retorts.

"I know he is a very gifted artist," Paul says, his tone soothing. "He has sold many of his works in the local shops. I know this. But he can be Amish for the family and an artist for himself."

Elizabeth turns around, and resumes slicing the bread. After a brief silence, she turns back around to face Paul. "Paul, you know very well that there is more to it than that."

Paul wipes his mouth with his napkin, folds it neatly, and places it on the table next to his plate. He sits back in his chair.

"Well that may be true, but he knows very well that he cannot be both with us and the 'English' woman. He has to choose."

"That's the problem. He's being pushed into a corner. He loves her, I'm sure. But he loves his family, too, and he worries that he may lose us. And I, for one, do not want to lose him. He's a good son," Elizabeth says with emotion filling her voice and her eyes starting to well up. She takes a tissue from her apron pocket and dabs at her eyes.

Paul stands up slowly from his chair. "I love my son like you do, but that does not change the fact that if he chooses to be with her, he will have to leave the farm and our way of life. The world out there is very difficult and filled with danger. I fear for him."

"Well, Paul, that's something he has to learn for himself," Elizabeth replies. "Unless he tries, he will always wonder if it could have been possible. And if he tries and fails, at least he will have no regrets about never trying."

Paul smiles and walks around the table to where Elizabeth is standing. He takes her hands in his. "You know something; for a tough farm girl, you have a big, soft heart." He hugs her close and presses his cheek against hers. "Now dry those tears. We will talk more about this later."

Elizabeth sniffles twice and wipes her now-very-red nose with her tissue. Paul kisses her on the forehead. He reaches for his hat, walks over to the kitchen door, and stops.

"That was a mighty fine breakfast. Thank you, love."

Then he puts on his hat and walks out the door.

It is the fall harvest, and all the farmers in the area are scrambling about in a sort of controlled frenzy to get the crops in before the first frost.

Like most other Amish farmers in Lancaster County, Pennsylvania, the Schaeffers grow a variety of crops. They grow corn, oats, rye, and hay for feeding their own livestock, which they cultivate primarily for their own consumption. Most of their income is earned by selling raw, whole milk to the region's large commercial dairies. Additional income is generated by growing "cash" crops, such as tomatoes and potatoes, which are sold to local grocery stores or directly to the public.

However, unlike many of the other Amish farmers in the area, the Schaeffer family does not grow tobacco. This anti-tobacco policy is Jonathan's handiwork. He, the reluctant farmer, represents the younger generation of more socially conscious Amish farmers.

Jonathan and his two younger brothers, Jacob, age fifteen, and Matthew, age eleven, are in the barn hooking up the plow horses to the harvester. Though these huge animals dwarf them, the boys appear to be in complete control as they skillfully maneuver the massively muscled horses into their harnesses.

Jonathan is directing his hard-working younger brothers, whose white shirts are already soaked with sweat.

Jonathan takes off his hat and wipes his forehead with a cloth. "All right now, boys, let's move them out. Jacob, you drive the cart. Matthew, hop in with me."

The boys scramble up to their positions.

Not far from Jonathan and his brothers, Paul is filling a large generator with gasoline. He turns to watch his three sons guide their horses to the fields. His first reaction is to smile and nod approvingly. But when he starts focusing on Jonathan in the distance, his mood turns somber.

The thought crosses his mind, as it often does, that someday Jonathan may decide to leave them, and the farm life, for the "English" girl. Paul has tried to prepare himself emotionally as best he can, should that day arrive. Of course, he wants Jonathan to choose, once and for all, the Amish ways; but he is fully aware that Vickie lives close by in New York City, and that her emotional pull on Jonathan remains strong and relentless.

And in his heart, Paul knows that Elizabeth is right when she argues that Jonathan has to make his own decision; a decision he will have to live with for the rest of his life.

Made up of three sons, two daughters, and their parents, the Schaeffer family is extremely close knit. However, one overriding issue constantly threatens to split Jonathan from the group. He fell in love with the "English" girl the first moment he set eyes on her.

They were each other's secret love for a long time, until they finally began dating as teenagers. From the very beginning, they never really tried to keep their relationship a secret. In fact, just about everybody in town knew about them, and with few exceptions, were accepting of their unusual friendship.

Vickie came close to not moving to New York to attend The Juilliard School of Music, because she feared that she would not be able to bear being away from him. In fact, her worst fears would later be realized. But in the end, when she did leave Jonathan in order to pursue her long-held dream of a singing career, it broke her heart.

Why Vickie ultimately left was the same old story. She knew that if she had given up her dream of attending Juilliard and becoming a singer in order to stay in Lancaster with Jonathan, she would later grow to resent him, and blame him. He agreed with her decision. They both knew that she had to move on and pursue her dreams, with or without him.

She had begged him to come with her. And though he kept postponing his own baptism, and thereby delaying becoming a full-fledged member of the Amish church, in order to be with her; he was still not yet ready to leave his family when that dreaded day finally came for her to move north to New York City.

Jonathan is fiercely loyal to and protective of his parents and siblings. When there is a loved one to defend, his pacifist teachings and beliefs fly right out the window. He especially adores his two-year-old sister, Rebecca, with her long curls and big, brown eyes. He cannot imagine not seeing her and hugging her every day.

And as it turns out, he cannot bear not seeing and hugging Vickie every day.

He continues to believe that, some day, they will get back together. He still hopes that he can have both the "English" girl and his family, and that ultimately, things will work out in the end somehow.

For the first year, they wrote each other every week. But as the weeks, months, and then years continued their inexorable march through time, the initial torrent of letters dwindled to a trickle, and then just stopped altogether. Perhaps it just became too painful for them to write the words in those letters. And then their phone conversations became more and more awkward and emotionally wrenching, until finally, they stopped, too.

Romantics like to believe that true love never dies. To this day, Jonathan still wakes up in the morning and goes to bed at night thinking about Vickie. Only when he drifts off to sleep at night does he find peace from his never-ending parade of thoughts of her, because until now, she has not yet invaded his dreams. Still, he is quite certain that these moments of freedom from his relentless thoughts of her will not last much longer, and that before long, she will come to haunt his dreams, just as she already haunts his days.

As Jonathan now guides the harvester through the corn fields, the horses pulling steady and sure, just as they have done countless times before, his thoughts carry him back six years in time.

CHAPTER II

"Hey, Mom, I've got to go into town," the sixteen-year-old Jonathan calls out as he skips down the stairs, jumping over the last three steps. He bursts into the kitchen and slides to a stop. He runs one hand through his hair, and with the other hand, slips a wide-brimmed straw hat onto his head.

Elizabeth looks up from the table where she is cutting carrots for the dinner stew. Her beautiful face is softly rounded.

"Jonathan, isn't it a little late to be going into town?" she asks with a frown, knowing full well that it is only four o'clock p.m. in July.

"Mom, you worry too much," Jonathan chides. "I'll tell you what; to save time, I'll just saddle up one of the horses…too much time to hook up the buggy."

"I don't like you riding horses on the road," Elizabeth counters. "The buggy is much safer."

"I'll be okay, Mom. I'll take the back roads…fewer cars that way."

He runs out the back door before she can respond. The screen door slams against the door jam. Elizabeth winces at the loud crack.

"Sorry about that, Mom. I'll be back before dinner," Jonathan yells out over his shoulder as he trots over to the barn.

The barn is located a short distance from the farmhouse. Typically red and cavernous, the barn was built only a few months ago. It was not that the old barn burned down, or anything quite as dramatic as that. The fact is that, under its countless coats of paint, the barn was rotting, and the horses and cows had banged and chewed it up pretty badly.

When the word spread that the Schaeffer family needed a new barn, the local Amish community organized a barn-raising for them. No one knows exactly how the word got out that the Schaeffers needed a new barn. It was probably an Amish neighbor who took notice of their dilapidated old barn, and thereby set in motion the whole barn-raising event. How it all happened does not matter. A fellow Amish farmer was in need of something considered vital to the family and farm, and so the need was fulfilled. No questions needed to be asked nor answered.

And it was not that the Schaeffers were too poor to build a new barn on their own, but it would have been a heavy financial burden for them to do so. Because the Schaeffers have shunned the growing and selling of tobacco, and because they have not branched outside of farming and into other businesses, such as construction; they are not as affluent as they could be. They are financially comfortable, but their budget is tight enough that without the goodwill of their neighbors, a new barn would have waited its turn near the bottom of a long priority list.

Being an experienced horseman, Jonathan takes little time to finish tacking his horse, a fourteen-year-old Appaloosa named Stormy, a name that, at first glance, seems not at all inspired by his disposition, as he stands there still as a statue, his eyelids drooping.

"Come on, boy, let's go," Jonathan commands, as he swings himself up into the saddle.

It usually takes a firm kick to get old Stormy moving, but once he gets going, Stormy is much admired for his long, smooth stride. In a moment, Jonathan and Stormy are off galloping towards town, with the lush rolling farmlands rising up in front of them.

This area of Pennsylvania is known as "The Garden Spot" of the country, because its soil is as fertile as any in the world. The region's rich farmland spreads out like a plush, green carpet, as far as the eye can see. A good portion of this land is now owned by Amish farmers.

Most of the Amish families in this region could be far more affluent than they are if they wanted to be. The land on which they farm has become extremely valuable, and they could become far wealthier just by selling off parcels of their land. But they do not own and work their farms in order to become rich. They embrace the farm life as a way of nurturing and supporting their families and communities. The farm is the key to maintaining their religious and cultural way of life.

Jonathan dismounts Stormy and ties him to a rail in the parking lot of the local stationary supplies store.

A middle-aged-looking woman walks by, and smiles. Jonathan smiles backs, and tips his hat.

He pats Stormy on his thickly muscled neck. "You be a good boy now until I get back." He turns and walks into the store.

As soon as he enters, it is instantly clear that Jonathan is something of a celebrity in this establishment.

"Hey, Jonathan, how's it going?" a store employee calls out from behind the register.

"Everything's fine, thank you," Jonathan answers back politely.

Jonathan is well known in these parts for his impeccable manners and quickness to help others, whether with some practical advice or just helping to load someone's car with bags of supplies.

Wherever he goes, Jonathan receives an almost embarrassing amount of attention, especially from women, young and old, Amish or not. He has chiseled symmetrical features, a strong jaw, broad shoulders, and bulging forearms; all of which explains why women flirt with him so shamelessly.

Most adult Amish males choose to maintain a decidedly low

profile. They do not want to be noticed beyond the unavoidable distinction of their clothes, hats, and beards. This is the way they like it.

On the other hand, young Amish men are far more outgoing, and are much more willing to wear their Germanic good looks with flair.

With a simple smile and a polite tip of his hat, Jonathan often, and not always unintentionally, elicits blushing in female passersby.

A young woman rushes up to him.

"Hi, Jonathan," she says, breathlessly. "May I help you today?"

He turns towards her. "Hi, Mary. Yes, thank you. Let me see... I need sketching paper, a pack of charcoal pencils, some water colors. But you really don't have to..."

"I'll get that for you," Mary blurts out, interrupting him. "I know just what you like."

Her face beginning to blush, she whirls around, and rushes down the aisle.

"Thank you, Mary," he says, as he smiles and tips his hat.

Jonathan walks over to a shelf filled with paint brushes, and starts looking them over.

A few minutes later, Mary heads over to the register with his supplies in hand. She firmly nudges another worker out of the way.

"Jonathan, I'll check you out here," she calls out.

Jonathan strides over to the counter. "Thanks for the help, Mary," he says.

"Don't mention it, Jonathan," she purrs.

After settling up, he thanks her again, tips his hat, and heads for the door.

"You're welcome, Jonathan," she calls out after him.

Looking like a deer in the headlights, she stares at him walking out of the store.

Jonathan has almost reached his horse when he hears a voice

that he knows well. When he turns and looks, a shiver shoots up his spine like an electrical pulse.

Now distracted, and with his head turned in the direction of the voice, he reaches up to grip the saddle horn. Just as he pulls his muscular six-foot frame up onto the saddle, Stormy shakes his head petulantly and stutter-steps sideways. This act of defiance quickly grabs Jonathan's attention.

"Whoa, boy," Jonathan shouts as he pulls back firmly on the reins with both hands.

Stormy comes to an abrupt halt.

"That's a good boy," Jonathan says soothingly, as if talking to a small child.

Now firmly back in control of the thousand-pound Stormy, Jonathan swings him around in the direction of the voice.

The subject of his interest is a sixteen-year-old girl of breath-taking beauty. Her softly rounded face is framed by long curls of light-brown hair. Her hair's naturally blond highlights contrast stunningly with her smooth, honey-colored complexion.

Jonathan sees tension in her fine-featured face, and he hears an urgency in her voice.

"What do you mean you don't know where he went? Mom, I can't believe you just let him take the car. I need to get home now. I have a very important rehearsal tonight."

Victoria Shaheen abruptly stops talking into her phone, and listens quietly to her mother on the other end.

"I'm not raising my voice to you, Mom." She listens some more. "Okay, I'll start walking, and if he shows up, please have him pick me up. I will, Mom. Don't worry, I won't. Yes, Mom. I love you, too. Bye." Flustered, Vickie sighs and angrily snaps the phone shut.

She starts fiddling in her bag for something, and as she does so, she happens to look up and see Jonathan across the parking lot, sitting on his horse, and looking right at her. Like every other teenage girl in town, she knows who he is. And like every other teenage girl in town at whom he looks, she feels her cheeks getting warm.

He starts walking his horse towards her.

"He's not coming over here, is he?" she asks out loud to herself.

He continues walking the horse straight towards her.

She now looks down into her bag, as if still fumbling for that something-or-other, and then looks up at him again.

"Oh, my God, he is coming over here," she whispers to herself, her cheeks now so flushed that they are tingling.

She shifts her heavy book bag to the other shoulder. She looks to the right, and then to the left, and then, not able to avoid him any longer, she looks right at him.

"Hello, Vickie," he says, a big smile on his face.

"Oh...hello...Jonathan," she stammers.

He crosses his hands over the saddle horn and leans down towards her. "I overheard you on the phone. Do you need some help?"

"Well, no, not really. Well, actually, yes. My ride is late, and I may be late for a rehearsal tonight."

He extends his hand. "Give me your book bag."

She stares at him for a moment, looking like she has absolutely no idea what he is talking about, her green brown eyes bigger than usual. But then, before she even realizes what she is doing, she finds herself hefting the heavy bag up towards him. And as the bag travels slowly upwards, she has time to ponder the fact that her mind has completely lost all control over what her arm is doing.

Jonathan reaches down and snatches the bag from her, like it is filled with air, and slings it over the front of the saddle. Then he reaches down again towards her. "Grab my hand."

Her already big eyes suddenly get much bigger. "What do you mean?"

"Vickie, grab my hand," he says again. "I'm taking you home."

"Oh, you are, are you?" she replies in a huffy little voice.

But her hand, like her arm, has also developed a mind of its own, because it starts floating up towards Jonathan. He wraps his powerful hand around her small, delicate hand and effortlessly pulls her up into the saddle in front of him.

"Swing your leg over, and hold on here," Jonathan says, as he places her hands on the saddle horn.

"I can't believe I'm doing this!" she gasps.

"I can," Jonathan replies. And with that said, he turns Stormy around, gives him a little kick, and off they go.

In the stationary store behind them, staring, open-mouthed faces adorn every window.

Vickie is holding on for dear life, her hair blowing in the wind as wildly as the pounding in her heart.

Vickie and Jonathan have had a crush on each other from the first time they laid eyes on each other. But until now, they have never done anything more with each other than exchange standard pleasantries.

After a mile or so down the road, a question suddenly pops into Vickie's mind, and she turns her body towards him.

"How do you know where I live?" she asks.

"How could I not know where you live?"

"What is that supposed to mean?"

Jonathan smiles.

Vickie frowns.

"Look, Jonathan, are you supposed to be doing what you're doing?"

"What am I doing, other than giving you a ride home?"

"Oh, come on, Jonathan. You know what I'm talking about. You're Amish. And I'm not."

"I know who you are, and what you are, and the only thing that matters to me is that you are Vickie Shaheen. And by the way, you're wrong, technically speaking. I'm not exactly Amish yet, technically speaking."

"Stop the horse! Stop the horse!" she commands.

He pulls back hard on the reins. Stormy stops on a dime.

Vickie turns around, grabs Jonathan's chin, and look him right in his eyes. "Look at me, Jonathan Schaeffer," she says. "Explain to me what you mean by…you're not Amish yet?"

For a moment, he loses himself in the sublime revelation that she knows his last name. Then he sees that Vickie is not smiling.

"Uh…listen, Vickie, you don't have to get all serious. You sure you want to get into this now?"

"I'm quite sure," she answers, her tone no nonsense.

"Okay, you asked for it," Jonathan says. "Well, let's see, the best way to explain it is that the Amish believe that its members must choose for themselves whether or not to join the church. They believe that this decision should be made only when the individual is mature enough to make such a decision. That's around sixteen years of age. Once the decision to join the Amish church is made, that individual then undergoes baptism. And only after baptism does one officially become a member of the Amish church."

"You mean to tell me that because you haven't been baptized yet, you're not officially Amish?"

"Yes, that's pretty much it in a nutshell."

Jonathan takes off his hat and wipes his brow with his hand. He takes a deep breath, and puts his hat back on.

Apparently bored by all the talk, Stormy snorts, lowers his head, and begins ripping at the tall grass growing along the side of the dirt road.

Jonathan presses on, trying his best to explain over three hundred years of cultural and religious history in a few brief sentences.

"Our belief in and practice of adult baptism are the main reasons the Amish people were branded heretics centuries ago in Europe, and persecuted and killed, often by being burned at the stake. The Amish were driven from one country to another. You see, in Europe back then, and even to this day, the dominant Christian religions believed in childhood baptism. The Amish came to this country nearly three hundred years ago because America, especially the Pennsylvania colony, offered them something Europe would not: freedom from religious persecution."

They sit in silence for a moment, as Stormy continues to tear up the roadside grass like any other thousand-pound weed whacker.

As for Vickie, it is not enough that this whole situation is more than a little surreal for her, but now she is trying to figure out who this guy is, and why she is here with him right now. Though she knows that she is not dreaming, she still feels compelled to pinch herself on the back of her arm. Although this guy has been the teenage heartthrob for most of the girls in town for several years now, it was always assumed by all the non-Amish girls that he was off-limits; a young Amish man who would eventually marry a plain but pretty Amish woman and have handsome, well-groomed, well-behaved, and plain Amish children.

To be sure, many of the young non-Amish, or "English," women in town would fantasize about Jonathan in many ways, some not always so pure, but none ever dared dream of actually being his girlfriend. To them, he might as well have been an alien from another planet.

These thoughts are now racing through Vickie's head like earth-rattling, Formula One race cars.

"Okay, now listen to me, Jonathan," she blurts out. "Are you saying that you and I could start dating each other?"

"Yes, I've wanted that for a long time."

"I've wanted that for a long time, too. I just never thought it was possible."

When she starts to say something else, he puts his finger on her lips and takes her face in his hands. Her eyes get real wide. He leans in and kisses her on the lips. For a moment, her eyes stay wide open, no doubt from the initial shock of being kissed by an Amish guy. Then, her eyelids slowly begin to close.

Lost in the kiss, she becomes disoriented and dizzy, and she starts swaying in the saddle. Jonathan reaches around the middle of her back with his arm and pulls her close.

After a long kiss, he slowly releases his hold around her.

"This must be a dream," she muses to herself, her eyelids still closed.

When she opens her eyelids, she sees that Jonathan is staring into her eyes.

"Is this some sort of dream?" she asks, a loopy smile on her face.

"It better not be," he replies. "But dream or not, I better get you home. Remember; your rehearsal."

This dose of reality snaps her back from gaga land.

She looks at her watch, blinks, and looks again. "Oh, my gosh, we better get going. I'm going to be so late."

"Don't worry; we'll get you home in no time. Hold on."

He gives Stormy a firm kick, and they take off, galloping down the road, with dirt kicking up behind them, and Vickie holding on for dear life.

As a marching band of thoughts and images passes through her spinning head, Vickie tightens her hold on the saddle horn.

Jonathan is holding the reins with both hands.

As Stormy picks up speed, Jonathan removes his hat, fearing that the wind might blow it off. His hair is now bouncing around wildly in the wind. In front of him, Vickie's hair is doing the same thing.

Townspeople are accustomed to seeing riders on horseback. But the sight of two people, one Amish and the other not, riding tandem is certainly cause for wonderment, if not bewilderment. Vickie is dreamily oblivious to their open-mouthed stares, while a smiling Jonathan nods and waves his hat, as they ride past the curious and the incredulous.

When they pull up in front of Vickie's house, the whole neighborhood stops to stare at them.

Jonathan jumps off the horse and ties the reins to a fencepost. He reaches up and helps Vickie down off the horse.

At first a bit unsteady, she holds on to Jonathan's arms for a moment before quickly regaining her bearings.

He removes her book bag from the saddle.

She looks at him. "Thank you for the ride," she says.

"It was my pleasure," he replies. "By the way, you should think about getting a smaller bag, or maybe a bigger shoulder," he adds as he carefully places the bag on her shoulder.

"I know. It's so ridiculous," she replies as she turns to look around. When she sees that the whole neighborhood is gawking at them, she lets out a soft gasp.

"Don't worry about them," Jonathan says calmly. "I've been stared at my whole life. I hardly notice it anymore. You'll get used to it, too, especially when you become a famous singer."

Vickie stops looking around, and turns back to him. "What makes you so sure that I'm going to become famous?"

"I've heard you sing."

"Where have you heard me sing?"

"In church."

"You've been to my church?"

"Many times."

"How could I have not noticed you in my church?"

"Because I was dressed in regular clothes, like what you 'English' wear," he replies matter-of-factly.

Though rarely at a loss for words, Vickie now finds herself standing in front of Jonathan, speechless.

Jonathan proceeds to put his hat on and adjust it to his liking. He then takes her hands in his, and gives them a gentle squeeze.

"We can talk more about this later. But now you've got to get going, or you're going to be really late."

He turns, lifts his foot into the stirrup, and swings himself up into the saddle.

Stormy snaps his sleepy head to attention.

Vickie snaps her dreamy head to attention. "When will I see you again?"

"Soon. Very soon. Stay alive. I will find you," he says, grinning. Then he pulls Stormy around, gives him a gentle kick, and off they go.

"He's been coming to my church to hear me sing all these years. Stay alive…I will find you. Isn't that a line in a movie? So he also sneaks around and watches movies. What else does that boy do?" Vickie wonders out loud.

She gazes after him for a few moments before looking around at no one in particular. Then she turns and walks up the brick walkway of her brightly painted home, with its neatly manicured yard. She opens the front door and disappears inside.

Only when the front door closes do the neighbors return to minding their own business.

Vickie's two younger siblings, Michael, age eight, and Lizzy, age six; and her mother, Veronica, are in the kitchen, all appearing to be busy making dinner. Vickie also has an older brother, Sam, age seventeen, who is missing in action with their mother's car.

However, Vickie cannot be too mad at Sam, because if it were not for his lack of consideration, her wild ride with Jonathan would never have happened. But because of Sam, she is going to be late for her rehearsal, so she will definitely have some choice words for him when he gets back with the car.

Vickie walks into the kitchen. She put her hands on her hips. "All right you guys, you can all stop pretending to be doing something."

They all stop what they are doing and look at her, innocently.

"Look, I saw all of you, including you, Lizzy, watching through the window."

Vickie bolts across the kitchen, snatches up her little sister, and starts swinging her around.

"Was that your boyfriend?" Lizzy asks, excitedly.

Vickie puts her down. "I don't know what all of you think is going on, but whatever you think it is, I'm not talking…yet."

"Did you guys kiss on the lips?" Michael asks mockingly, puckering his lips.

Vickie charges towards Michael. "I'll show you a kiss, right on your bare butt with my bare hand."

Squealing with delight, Michael takes off running.

Vickie starts to run after him, but then stops suddenly and looks over at her mother, who is half-smiling, at best.

Michael's muffled voice can be heard coming from the family room.

"You better hide, little boy, cause if I get ahold of you…" Vickie yells out.

Vickie turns back to her mother. "Stop worrying, Mom. I'll explain things later. I can't talk right now. I'm already late for rehearsal."

Her mother just looks at her, saying nothing.

"Mom, is that okay? Can we talk later?" Vickie implores.

When her mother finally speaks, she enunciates each word

slowly. "Okay, Victoria, but we really must talk later."

"I know. I know. We will," Vickie promises as she turns and rushes upstairs to her bedroom.

A few minutes later, a car pulls into the driveway of Vickie's home. A teenage girl is driving. She beeps the horn twice.

Still brushing her hair, Vickie runs out of her bedroom and down the stairs. "I'll be home right after rehearsal."

Her mom follows right behind her. "What time is that, young lady?"

"About ten," she yells out, as she runs down the front walkway.

"I want you home before your father gets home from the airport."

"Don't worry, Mom. I will be."

She then hops into the front passenger seat. The car backs out of the driveway, turns, and heads down the road.

Vickie's mother, Veronica, who is African-American, and like her daughter, stunningly beautiful, watches from the window as the girls drive away. Clearly, she does not look happy about much of anything right now.

The car carrying Vickie and her friend pulls up to an old warehouse in a rundown, industrial neighborhood, consisting of several blocks of empty decaying buildings and vacant lots filled with trash piles, overgrown weeds, high grass, and bracken.

Vickie's friend, Lisa, parks her car at the curb in front of the building. A sign on the front of the building reads "Clearnotes Recording Studio."

Vickie looks around before opening the car door. "Why are recording studios always located in the worst part of town?"

"I don't know, maybe it's a conspiracy to weed out all the wannabe singers, leaving only the most committed ones like us," Lisa answers, sarcastically.

"Committed? We should be committed for coming into an area like this," Vickie snorts, as she steps out of the car.

They walk up to the front door. Vickie rings the buzzer.

A voice crackles from the intercom speaker. "Yeah?"

Vickie leans in close to the speaker. "It's Vickie and Lisa."

The door buzzes obnoxiously.

They both push the heavy door open as quickly as possible, if only to shut up the buzzer.

As soon as they walk into the studio's front lobby, the girls feel infused with a burst of energy.

"I love this place," Vickie coos.

"Me too," Lisa purrs.

A scruffy young man is sitting behind the front desk, talking on the telephone.

He shuffles through a schedule book. "Look, Jerry, I'll put you in studio three for Thursday at nine p.m. But if I'm going to do you this favor, you can't cancel on me again, dude. Are we clear on that? Okay, partner. We'll see you then."

He puts the phone down and looks up at Vickie. "Hi, Vic. You're late."

"I know. I'm sorry. I have an excuse, but it's a long story," Vickie replies.

"Spare me the details. You guys are in studio two tonight. Chop, chop."

"Thanks, Rick," Vickie says, sweetly.

As they walk down the long, brightly lit hallway, with its walls covered with colorful posters, and blown up photographs of singers, musicians, and musical groups, every person they pass by smiles and says hi. This is a happy place, no doubt.

No matter how foul her disposition might be, when Vickie walks into this oasis in the desert, her mood changes quickly, and for the better.

They reach the door to studio two. Lisa pushes open the door, and the two girls walk into a large room. A raised, hardwood stage sits at one end of the rehearsal room.

Next to the stage, four musicians are busy setting up their instruments. The band's leader, Jim, is bent over the electric keyboards, adjusting buttons and dials.

He looks up at the girls. "Hello, ladies. How are you doing?"

Vickie walks towards him. "We're doing fine. And how are you guys doing?"

"We're all doing great, babe, and you girls are late," Jim says.

"It's my fault, Jim. Not Lisa's," Vickie quickly explains.

"Listen, kids, I don't want to hear any excuses. We don't have the time. We've got a lot of work to do tonight, and not much time to do it. We've got to be out of here by ten p.m."

"I've got to be home by then," Vickie says out loud to herself.

Jim continues. "I'm not happy with some of the vocal arrangements. Also, I want to try out some new things tonight. So let's get your voices warmed up and get started as soon as possible."

Jim hands both girls a stack of sheet music. "Look these over. If you have any questions, let me know," he says as he points them to the other side of the room. "You girls go on over there now and start getting ready. Thank you, ladies."

In his late twenties, Jim is well known in the area as a very accomplished keyboardist, and an even more talented arranger.

Vickie is the newest member of the group. Six months ago, she learned that Jim's band was holding auditions for a female lead singer. At the time, her reputation in the community as an extremely talented young vocalist was rapidly growing. She was a principal singer in her church choir, and the lead singer in the madrigal singing group at her high school.

As her reputation grew, so did the crowd at the church where she sang every Sunday.

At first, Jim was a little worried about her young age, but when he and the band members heard her sing at the audition, they almost fell out of their chairs.

Vickie's voice has perfect pitch, a very rare quality in pop singers of today. Her vocal range is a true four octaves. Furthermore, her voice shows no distortion whatsoever at either end of her octave range. And her versatility is such that she sings equally well in virtually all the musical genres, especially those in which the ability to sing on key is still a valued and required quality, such as classical pop, R&B, jazz, and classical.

At her audition for the band, as soon as she sang her first verse, Jim and the other band members knew immediately that Vickie had the potential to be a superstar. Any doubts they had regarding her young age evaporated when she sang a medley of "oldies but goodies." Her style was so polished, and her phrasing so precise, that they could not believe that she was only fifteen years old.

The band is made up of four very talented guys, who simply have not had that "lucky break." Jim plays the keyboard and sings backup. Ronnie plays lead guitar, Steve is the drummer, and Chris sings backup and plays the bass guitar. Lisa sings backup and sometimes performs duets with Vickie. But it is Vickie who has quickly become the star of the group, a fact no one in the band disputes.

"Okay everybody," Jim calls out, as he settles down on the stool in front of the keyboards, "Let's get started."

As they walk over to their positions behind the standing microphones, Vickie turns to Lisa. "I hope I don't mess up."

"I heard that," Jim says, smiling. "And you know what…I hope we don't all mess up."

Vickie is now beginning to feel that tingling of excitement and wave of anxiety that she has learned to expect, and even welcome, before each and every performance, whether it is just a rehearsal or the real thing. She has always loved singing and performing, especially in front of a live audience.

Just as Vickie is stepping up to the studio microphone, Jonathan is opening the barn door. Stormy walks obediently into his stall.

Jonathan immediately begins brushing him down. The old Appaloosa is standing very still. Sweat glistens on his white and brown coat. Though Stormy always loves a good run, and is much admired for his speed and stamina, typical of his breed, the long ride with two riders on his back has left him exhausted.

Jonathan brings him a bucket of water. Stormy wastes little time in sucking the bucket dry. Never too tired to eat, Stormy starts gulping down his evening flake of hay just as soon as Jonathan lays it on the floor of his stall. Jonathan then slices several apples into wedges and places them and a few carrots in his feeding bucket. He gives Stormy a final pat on his thickly muscled neck.

"Enjoy yourself, old boy. You deserve it. You did real well today."

Jonathan walks up to the back door of the house.

His family is already sitting around the table. The dinner food sits in platters and bowls on the table in front of them. Like Stormy, the Schaeffers are tired and hungry. But no matter how hungry they might be, they will not start dinner until Jonathan joins them at the table.

As soon as he walks through the kitchen door, they all turn and look at him.

"I bet you're all hungry as the dickens," Jonathan says, looking around at everyone sitting at the table. "I'm sorry I kept you all waiting. I have a pretty good reason."

"It's okay. Come on now. Hurry up. Sit down. We can discuss it later," Paul says impatiently, fork in hand.

Jonathan hangs his hat on a hook in the wall, pulls out a chair, and sits down with the family.

In short order, the Schaeffers turn their full attention to the food sitting on the table, and begin passing around bowls filled with salad greens and cooked vegetables, plates stacked with baked chicken, whole potatoes, and home-made bread warm from the oven. The only sounds heard now are the chomping and gulping sounds of six hungry folks. Little Rebecca is destined to make it seven hungry Schaeffers four years hence.

With a blink of his eyes, Jonathan awakens himself from his daydream. He looks around like someone lost in the woods. He is still holding the reins firmly in his grasp, while the plow horse is still pulling his load, straight and steady. The boys are in position. Everything is in its place. It is as if time has stood still.

He puts both reins in one hand, reaches into his back pocket with his other hand, and removes a small leather wallet. He opens it, and removes a small photograph of Vickie. He stares at her picture. It stares back at him.

CHAPTER III

Vickie is staring at her reflection in the dressing room mirror. A picture of Jonathan sits on the side of the dressing table. She glances at his picture, takes a deep breath, and starts brushing her golden-brown hair with long, lethargic strokes.

"This is the last time I'm doing this myself. I swear I'm getting a hairstylist from now on," she grumbles to herself.

From behind her, a voice calls out, "Five minutes, Vickie."

"Okay, Mike. I'll be ready in two," she yells out. Her long, slow brushstrokes quickly become short, fast strokes.

A minute later, she lays down the brush. As a young woman of dazzling natural beauty, Vickie has little need for makeup. All she ever needs is a little lip gloss and a bit of mascara and she is ready to take the stage.

She slides her chair back from the dressing table and stands up, steals another glance at Jonathan's picture, leans into the mirror to check her teeth for lipstick smears, and with the stylistic flourish of a dancer, whirls away from the mirror and rushes from the dressing room.

The band members have gathered behind the curtains at the side of the stage. They turn towards Vickie as she approaches them.

"Hey, beautiful," Jim calls out to her.

"Hi, guys," Vickie replies.

She walks up to Jim and gives him a hug. She then walks over to the other three band members and gives each of them a kiss on the cheek.

"Are you guys ready?" she asks.

"You bet, we're ready," Jim responds.

Vickie claps her hands twice. "I am so excited and nervous tonight. I can't stand it."

Jim smiles and puts his arm around her shoulders. "That's always a good sign, sweetheart. You're going to knock them dead tonight."

Although the truth is that Vickie has become the knock-out star of the group and the reason for the band's worldwide success, she quickly brushes off any mention of this fact, and she never fails to praise her band members whenever the opportunity arises. Each of the guys in the group truly adores her, is amazed by her humility and generosity, is in awe of her talent, and would take a bullet for her.

Vickie and the guys have been led to the wings of the amphitheater at Jones Beach in Queens, New York. They are standing, huddled close together, talking quietly.

When the announcer begins to introduce them to the sold-out audience, they grow silent.

The crowd, which has grown restless, begins to clap and whistle, even before he finishes his introduction. The fans have waited patiently through two opening acts, both of which were top notch. But now they are primed and ready for the headliners.

The stage manager walks up to Vickie and her band members. "Let's now get each of you to your position," he says calmly.

The guys stroll onto the stage and over to their instruments. Each one may look cool and calm on the outside, but on the inside, each musician is vibrating with anticipation and nervous energy.

Vickie walks over to her position behind the microphone. She closes her eyes, bows her head, and stands very still.

Just as the announcer finishes his introductory words, the curtain slowly begins to rise.

Vickie and her band are standing motionless; only their backlit silhouettes are visible on the darkened stage.

The crowd erupts in a deafening roar.

Suddenly, the spotlights flash on.

Vickie raises her head, and grabs the microphone off its stand. "Hello, New York!"

The crowd roars back.

Vickie strides to the front edge of the stage. "Are you having a good time?"

"Yes!" the crowd yells.

She struts over to the left side of the stage. "I'm sorry. I can't hear you, New York! Let me ask you again. Are you having a good time?"

"Yes!" the crowd roars back.

"You know that's music to my ears," Vickie shouts out.

She turns to Jim and nods. He turns to the band and nods. The band erupts into a rendition of their latest hit record. These musicians sound every bit as good in a live performance as in a studio recording, a true rarity in this age of multimillion dollar musical mediocrities.

Vickie strides back to the center of the stage and places the microphone back on the stand. She leans in close to the microphone and begins singing.

Her velvety soprano voice surrounds and engulfs the audience. The fans settle back in their seats, knowing from those first few soaring notes that this is going to be one of those really special nights of live entertainment that are so rare in this era of flash and no substance, in which bad singing, bad music, and bad songs have become the accepted norm in music entertainment. Pop music has become a strange world in which the lesser the musical and vocal talent, the bigger the glory and paycheck. Vickie is a throwback to the old days when singers sang real notes on key, in songs of great musical and lyrical beauty. She has become a bona fide star. Her records go platinum as soon as they hit the record stores. Her live concerts sell out within hours of the tickets going on sale.

But despite all of her success, there is something still missing. A melancholy hangs over her like a stubborn fog. She cannot, and will not, get over Jonathan. Thoughts and memories of him constantly haunt her reality. When she performs, she often finds herself looking for him in the audience. And whenever she sings a heart-searing torch song, she may be performing for the audience, but she is singing for Jonathan.

She often fantasizes that one day, after a show, once the applause has long faded away, she will open her dressing room door, and Jonathan will be standing there in the middle of the room. And he will walk over to her, lift her up in his arms, and spin her around and around, or so the fantasy goes.

The truth is, she knows that the odds of them ever getting back together are growing slimmer with each passing day. They have not even spoken to each other for almost a year now, and therein is the reason for her endless melancholy. Still, against all odds, she hopes for that fairytale ending.

Later that evening, after the Jones Beach concert, Vickie is sitting in the backseat of her stretch limousine.

Tony, her driver and bodyguard, glances back at her through the rearview mirror. Her head is resting on the back of her seat. Her small feminine hands sit folded on her lap. Her eyelids may be closed, but she is far from asleep.

It is virtually impossible for an entertainer to sleep immediately after a live performance. The adrenaline high lasts for hours after every performance. This is a major reason why so many performers turn to drugs and alcohol. At first, the chemicals are used for relaxation and to facilitate sleep. However, all too often for many entertainers, the drugs and alcohol become an escape from the pressures and anxieties associated with celebrity. And then, finally and tragically, the use of these chemicals becomes a career-and-life-destroying addiction, and a freefall to the bottom of a dark abyss.

Vickie puts no chemicals into her body. She goes home to her apartment on the upper west side of Manhattan, alone. She shuns after-show parties and is rarely ever seen at celebrity gatherings. Her band members have learned to accept the fact that she is a homebody who does not drink or smoke. When not performing or recording, her idea of a good time is to lounge around her spacious and tastefully decorated penthouse, reading biographies and romance novels, and listening to jazz and classical music. This is her method of escaping the relentless pressures of an international singing career.

She is not fond of listening to other singers, particularly the female ones.

Curled up on her bed, Vickie cuts a sensual and voluptuous figure. She stays fit and toned with a regimen of moderate exercise and dietary good sense. She watches what she eats, but she is far from fanatical about it.

Apart from her hectic and typically surrealistic life as an international singing star, she prefers to keep her life as uncomplicated as possible. The things in her life that she values most are her family and hard work; the same values held most dear by that ubiquitous object of her obsession, Jonathan.

In her moments of solitude, which are many, she thinks a lot about Jonathan. Staying connected to him helps to keep her grounded in the real world, a not so easy task for a young woman who exploded onto the world stage like a rocket on the fourth of July, and who quickly found fame and fortune beyond her wildest dreams.

Now stretched out on her bed, and propped up on a giant pillow, Vickie is trying her best to read at least one chapter of her latest romance novel before falling asleep. She is battling to stay awake, blinking each time her eyes begin to slip out of focus.

Finally, she is just too tired to fight sleep any longer. Her eyelids close slowly, and she quickly slips into a deep slumber. A smile forms on her face as dream sleep envelops her. Her dream carries her back four years in time to Lancaster, Pennsylvania.

Jonathan and Vickie, both eighteen years old, are lying side by side on their backs on a blanket in a freshly cut field of maize, gazing up at the nighttime sky.

Vickie's head is resting on his arm. She holds one of his hands in both of hers.

Tonight's sky is cloudless. The stars shine so brilliantly that they seem close enough to touch. A light breeze caresses their faces. Vickie shivers slightly from the chill in the air. She turns towards Jonathan and puts her arm around his chest.

He looks at her. Her face is glowing in the starlight. He then turns and nods at the stars. "You're going to be a star someday, just like those up in that sky."

She squeezes his hand. "I don't know about that. But what I do know is that right now I'm really afraid."

"Afraid of what?" Jonathan asks, knowing full well what she is talking about.

"You know darn well what I'm talking about," she says, as she buries her head in his chest.

"You're not going to lose me."

"But I want you to come with me, Jonathan."

"I know. I want to be with you, too, but…" He pauses.

She lifts her head off his chest and looks right at him. "I'm not asking you to leave your family. I know how important your family is to you. Coming with me to New York City is not leaving your family, Jonathan."

He sighs. "I'm just not as brave as you."

"It's not about being brave. It's about making a commitment to each other. I need you, and I don't know if I can do this without you."

"Believe me; I need you just as much."

Vickie sits up. "You know I have to go New York. I can't stay here."

"In my head, I know you have to go. But in my heart, I keep hoping for a miracle."

Vickie starts talking fast, her voice rising. "There's nothing wrong with your head or your heart. But you know that I need to leave this town. And so do you. New York City is the best place for someone with your talents. You will be very successful there. I know it."

Jonathan sits up, too. "I measure success in terms of the health and welfare of my loved ones. Fame and fortune don't hold much weight with me."

Vickie grabs him by his hand. "We both care very much about the health and welfare of our loved ones. And I'm not talking about fame and fortune. But we still have to live the lives that will bring us the greatest happiness. And your family will always love you and be there for you, no matter what you decide to do. And you will always be there for them. I know your mother believes this. I know how she thinks. And your father will also come around to supporting your decision. He is a very wise man. He just worries about his oldest son."

Vickie takes a deep breath.

There is a long silence.

"Look, you may be the strong, silent type, but I know this whole thing is gnawing away at you," Vickie finally says.

When Jonathan stays silent, looking straight ahead, Vickie jumps up to her feet, puts her hands on her hips, and looks down at him. "I will wait for you, Jonathan Schaeffer. I will wait for you for a good long while. But I will not wait forever."

Jonathan stands up and steps towards her. He grabs her, pulls her close, and whispers in her ear.

"I will always love you, too, no matter what happens," she says back to him, her voice breaking, as tears, glimmering in the moonlight, start chasing each other down her cheeks.

As Vickie buries her face into his shoulder, Jonathan gazes out over the darkened Pennsylvania countryside, where car lights flicker in the distance, and the shimmering full moon hovers just above the nearby treetops, and their gracefully swaying limbs.

Vickie's eyes open slowly.

Every light is on in the bedroom. The room is silent.

She sits up in bed and looks down at the book lying open on her lap. She hears a loud crack, and reaches for the back of her neck. "Oh, my neck," she groans.

Leaning forward, she starts massaging her neck and rolling her head around, first in one direction, and then in the other.

She pushes herself up off the bed and shuffles into the bathroom. Through half-closed eyes, she fills a glass with cold water from the water cooler in her bathroom, and then looks at her reflection in the mirror, at first not really focusing.

As she sips at the cold water, she is struck by how soothing the water is to her apparently parched throat. Not much of a water drinker, she takes a few more sips, pours the rest of the water into the sink, and walks back into the bedroom.

She stops in the middle of her bedroom and starts looking around. Before long, her eyes light up, and a big smile forms on her face. Her friends are smiling back at her. Her teddy bears sit in repose everywhere: in her bedroom, on the chairs, the couch, the chaise longue, the dresser, the mantel, everywhere. She knows that each and every bear is here in her bedroom for one reason, and one reason only…each bear spoke to her, and very politely asked to be taken home with her. If the teddy does not speak to her, the teddy stays on the store shelf. Simple as that.

A loud ring startles her.

Normally, the sound of the phone ringing is very annoying to her, but not tonight. Tonight, for some reason, she actually welcomes the obnoxious ringing. And so with unexpected anticipation, she picks up the phone.

"Hello."

"Victoria?"

"Yes," she replies.

"It's Michael."

"Michael, how are you?" she asks sweetly. The tingling of excitement resonating throughout her body surprises her.

"I'm fine, thank you. I didn't wake you, did I?"

"No, you didn't. I just got up. I fell asleep reading my book."

"Hey, you know, that's sounds pretty exciting," Michael replies.

Vickie sighs. "I know. My life can be pretty boring a lot of the time. But I like it like that."

"You're a smart woman. When you're not performing, you keep things simple. It gives you a chance to recharge your batteries. Don't change the way you are, and you're going to be around a long time, with your beautiful, boring self."

"Well, you know, flattery will get you everywhere."

"Will it get me a dinner date with you for tomorrow?"

Normally, Vickie would beg off, but not this time, not tonight. She answers without hesitation. "Well, yes, I believe it will."

Though surprised as can be, Michael stays calm. "All right,

doll," he says, in his best cool voice. "I'll pick you up at eight o'clock."

"I'll be ready. See you tomorrow,"

"Yes, we'll see you tomorrow. You enjoy that book now. But be sure to get your beauty sleep. Goodnight, now," Michael replies, his voice still low and sexy, belying the fact that he can barely hear his own voice over the pounding of his heartbeat.

"Goodnight, Michael."

Click.

Michael Stevens has been trying to get Vickie out on a date for a long time, but she has always politely declined, using one excuse or another.

Michael is tall, lean, and immaculately groomed. He is one of those really good-looking guys who men envy and women love. He has a reputation for being a real gentleman; the old-fashioned kind who still opens doors for women. Michael is a guy who knows how to compliment a lady without sounding like a player. And though he breaks a lot of hearts along the way, he always does it in such a gentlemanly way that women still keep flocking to him, like kittens to milk.

Michael is an executive in a record company, but not Vickie's label. To be sure, some day he would love to snatch her away from them. But for now, he will have to settle for just snatching her.

As for Vickie, she, too, has had her eyes on him for a while now. She first met him at one of those industry parties that she hates to attend, but must. Upon first meeting him, she felt that he seemed too smooth; too cocky. But as she got to know him better, she began to see him in a different light.

She came to know that, behind a veneer of business toughness, Michael is a kind and generous man in his personal life. In fact, he helps to support a large extended family. He is especially fond of his nephews and nieces. When he visits them, which is quite often, they swarm over "Uncle Mike" like bear cubs. He loves this.

On the other hand, in matters related to the music business, he is as hard as nails and can be ruthless, if necessary. However, his true nature is not to be heartless. And for this reason, he has a profound dislike for the music industry. He finds no pleasure in taking advantage of young musicians and singers; of exploiting their desperation to succeed.

But this is his job, and he is one of the best at it. The sad fact is that his drive to succeed in the music industry remains stronger than his desire to do something else better-suited to his inherently good nature. Michael knows full well that he must maintain his reputation for being a hard-nosed negotiator, because in his world, the weak get chewed up and swallowed by the sharks that swim in the cold and choppy waters of the soulless music industry.

As for his interest in Vickie, he is pretty sure that it is driven by something much more than her great beauty and vast talent. Perhaps he sees in her what is good and real and honest in people. He may even view Vickie as his salvation.

Still, he remains unsure of his own intentions towards her. He has yet to figure out for himself if his interest in her is personal, or professional, or both. The only thing of which he is certain is that, for a long time now, he has wanted to have her, hold her, and kiss her. And then at some point in the future, if he is still in the miserable music business, perhaps he can sign her to a new contract with his own record label.

The evening of the next day, and hardly able to contain his excitement, Michael finds himself ringing her doorbell at 7:30 pm, thirty minutes early. Fiddling nervously with his coat, and looking down at his shoes, he looks like a teenage boy standing at his date's front door on prom night.

Still in her bathrobe, Vickie opens the door. "Michael, you're early."

He looks up and is stunned. "Wow, you look amazing tonight."

She smiles. "Thank you, Michael. And you look very handsome tonight, as always. Please come in. Sit down and relax. Would you like something to drink?"

"No thanks. Look, I know I'm early, but I just couldn't wait any longer," Michael confesses.

"That's okay. I'm almost ready anyway. Just give me a few more minutes."

"Don't hurry. Take your time, take your time. I'll just sit down over there," Michael says, pointing to the sofa.

Michael walks over to the sofa and plops down on it. He unbuttons the top button of his shirt, takes a handkerchief from his pants pocket, and daps at the beads of sweat forming on his brow. He shakes his head and chuckles out loud to himself. "I can't believe how nervous I am. I feel like a kid on his first date."

"Did you say something, Michael?" Vickie calls out from the bedroom.

"No, everything is fine," he calls back. But, under his breath, he continues talking to himself. "Everything is fine all right. I'm sweating like a pig. My heart is trying to do an *Alien* out of my chest. I'm hyperventilating like a bride in an arranged marriage. Other than that, yeah, I'm great, just perfect."

He tries to focus on the music playing in the room. He recognizes Maurice White's voice on the Earth, Wind and Fire song, "Love's Holiday." He starts singing along to the lyrics.

Moments later, Vickie walks into the room, wearing a strapless black dress that appears to have been spray painted onto her hour glass figure. Her dancer's legs form a perfect curve into her small ankles. Her manicured toes, small and perfect, peek out from the front of wispy black high heels.

He swallows hard, and stands up. "You look amazing. I already said that, didn't I?"

She smiles. "Thank you, Michael. Are you ready to go?"

"I sure am," Michael says.

He takes her arm, and walks with her slowly to the front door. Vickie is walking very carefully towards the door, looking unsteady in her three-inch heels. Just as she reaches the door, her ankle turns over, and she stumbles forward. Michael grabs her by the waist, and holds her up.

"These darn shoes," Vickie grumbles, looking more than a little embarrassed.

"Are you okay?" Michael asks.

"Yes, thank you. As you can see, I haven't had a lot practice with shoes like these."

"Well, you look unbelievable in them."

"Yeah, sure, unbelievably clumsy," she replies.

Michael curls her arm around his. "Let's go eat. I bet all this exercise has given you quite an appetite."

"Actually, I'm starving," Vickie admits, as she gets a firm hold on his arm.

"I believe that."

Moments later, arms locked, they walk out the front door of the apartment building, down the stairs, and into a sleek black sedan.

Michael and Vickie are sitting across from each other at a small, round table covered with a white linen tablecloth. A tall, white candle and a single white rose in a slender, cut-glass vase sit on the table. Around them, patrons are talking quietly. The waiters are impeccably dressed, as they hover unobtrusively around the table. This bistro is very pricey, but one would never know it from its understated elegance.

"What do you feel like tonight?" Michael asks as he scans the menu, a fusion of French and Asian cuisine.

"I don't know. I always have such trouble deciding what to order. I'm kind of old fashioned. I want to try new things, but then I'm never happy when I do."

"My suggestion to you is to order what you're familiar with, and not worry about trying some exotic new dish that you probably will not like," Michael advises as he takes a sip of wine.

"Well, then, I know what I want," Vickie announces, looking happily relieved.

The waiter appears out of nowhere. "Are you ready to order, Mademoiselle?"

"Yes, thank you. I sure am. I'll have the field greens salad with goat cheese, and the free-range roasted chicken."

"Very good choices, Mademoiselle," the waiter says. He then turns to Michael. "And you, Monsieur?"

Michael orders his meal, and the waiter bows and departs.

Michael takes one of her hands and cradles it in both of his. "I can tell from what you ordered that you are a bit of a country girl."

"Is that a bad thing?" she asks innocently.

Michael leans in close to her. "I like you just the way you are."

With Michael so close, Vickie cannot help but notice that his breath smells like fresh mint leaves. She finds this aroma very pleasing. Then her gaze moves to his hands. She notices that his fingers are long and slender, and that his nails are perfectly manicured. Her thoughts begin to linger on the image of a man having his nails manicured in a nail salon. She tries mightily to block out of her mind any negative thoughts of about this, but Michael's fingernails stick in her mind. And soon, she finds herself helplessly wondering about his toenails, and if they too are manicured in a nail salon.

"A penny for your thoughts," Michael says to Vickie, with a sweet smile on his face.

Vickie blinks. "Oh, I'm sorry, Michael. I was just thinking about how hungry I really am right now. I may tear into that chicken with my bare hands."

Michael ponders the notion of tearing into her with his bare hands.

"It'll be a pleasure watching a woman actually eat a meal for a change and not just pick at it," Michael replies, a naughty grin on his face.

"Oh, I enjoy eating. You'll never see me sticking my fingers down my throat after a meal," is what Vickie says to Michael. But what she is thinking is, "Picking at my food is exactly what I usually do. What do you think...I'm going to eat like a Clydesdale?"

Michael leans back. "Well, that's good to know," he chuckles.

Vickie is looking right into his eyes and smiling. He smiles back at her, and takes another sip of wine.

The black sedan pulls up in front of her apartment building on West Seventy-Second Street.

The driver gets out and opens the curbside door. Always the gentleman, Michael gets out first and helps Vickie out of the car.

He takes her arm, and together, they walk into the building.

He stands behind her in the hallway as she opens her apartment door. She reaches in, turns on the light, and walks into the room. He follows her in. She walks over to a chair in the entry and puts her purse down on the seat.

When she turns around, he is standing right in front of her.

She starts to say something, but he places his fingertips on her lips. She looks up at him with her big eyes. He looks right into them. An electrical impulse shoots up her spine and into the back of her neck.

He takes her face in his hands and kisses her gently on the lips. An electrical impulse shoots up his spine and into the back of his neck.

He pulls her closer and presses his lips against hers. Feeling her knees getting weak, she grabs him around the neck, more to keep from falling down than from passion, though there is that, too.

He reaches down and lifts her into his arms. She gives a little gasp. Her toes point involuntarily as he carries her over to the couch and lays her down. He sits down next to her and begins kissing her on the neck, first on the side, and then around to the front.

She leans her head back against the sofa, her eyes closed, and her lips parted slightly. Michael works his way down towards her chest. She arches her back and places her hand on the back of his head.

His hand starts sliding down towards her hip.

Suddenly, her eyes open wide. "Michael!"

"Vickie!"

Vickie looks down at the top of his head. "Michael!" she says again, but louder.

"Oh, Vickie!" he says again, with even more passion.

Vickie grabs his face with both hands, and lifts up his head. "Stop, Michael, now!" she commands.

"What?"

"I said stop, Michael," she repeats, her tone less harsh.

Looking a lot like a child who has just been admonished, Michael sits straight up. "I'm sorry, Vickie. I thought you wanted to..."

Vickie interrupts him. "I do, but not yet," she explains, her tone now much softer. "Things were moving too fast, Michael. I want us to slow down. That's all."

Michael takes a deep breath and leans back against the sofa. "Oh, hey, I'm cool with that," he says. "There's no hurry, babe. You just let me know when you're ready."

She detects a certain tone in his voice. "Please don't be angry, Michael. I find you to be an extremely attractive man in many ways. Just be patient with me."

He lifts her hands to his lips, and kisses first one, and then the other.

An uncomfortable pause ensues.

Vickie breaks the silence. "What are you thinking, Michael? I can't read your mind."

Michael looks straight ahead. "Look, Vickie, I know this probably has something to do with that farm boy of yours back home."

Vickie looks stunned. "How do you know about him?" she asks, in a tone now harsh again.

"I've known about him as long as I've needed to know about him."

"What is that supposed to mean?"

"Look, Vickie, you know how things work in this business. My job is to know everything and anything important about not only my own artists, but also those working for the competition."

"You mean to say that you delve into the personal lives of people who may, in fact, value their privacy," Vickie says indignantly.

"You know that there is no such thing as a private life when you're in this business. And anyone in this business who can't handle that fact is in the wrong business. Hey, there's always graduate school, you know," Michael retorts sarcastically.

Vickie and Michael are doing their best to sound angry, but neither one is very convincing.

Vickie grows quiet. As upsetting and frustrating as it is, she knows Michael is only telling the truth. And so her indignation quickly melts into resignation.

"I was going to tell you about him when the time was right," she says meekly.

"Well, maybe now is the time," Michael suggests.

She puts her hand on his knee. "I'm just not ready to talk about him. Not yet."

He places his hand on her hand. "Why?"

"Because it would mean closing that chapter in my life, and to be honest with you, I'm not sure that chapter is over. I'm not sure that I want that chapter to be over."

She stands up and walks over to the chair where Michael's coat is draped. She lifts it off the chair and turns to him. "And by the way, there's nothing wrong with him being a farmer. His connection with the earth is one reason he is such an amazing artist."

Michael gets up from the couch. "I know about him being an artist. In fact, I've seen some of his works."

"Well, I'm not surprised," Vickie replies. "It is your business to know these things."

She opens his coat. "I've got a very busy day tomorrow in the studio."

Michael smiles and slowly walks over to her. He knows he is getting the boot, though gentle it may be.

"We're recording a song for the new album tomorrow," she adds. Just as soon as these words leave her mouth, she regrets them, because now Michael is going to ask her about the album.

Michael narrows his eyes. "How's that second album coming anyway?" he asks as he takes his coat from her.

"Things are going very well, thank you."

"Oh, really? I heard that it's been a little slow."

Vickie is caught off guard again. "Is there anything you don't know?" she asks, with a weak smile.

"In our business, there better not be," Michael replies nonchalantly as he puts his coat on.

Vickie looks down. "Well, Michael, you know how it can be with second albums. I hate the term 'creative block,' but I guess that's a large part of the problem. But I'm working through it, slowly but surely."

"You know, Vickie, that unresolved personal issues can be a real drag on some artists," Michael says in an almost paternal tone. "No matter what people think or say, the truth is that very few musicians and songwriters thrive on misery and heartache. Music is supposed to make us happy. But if the musician is not happy, it's going to be real hard for that person to write good music. Do you know what I mean?"

Vickie sighs. "Is it really that obvious?"

Michael points to a book lying open on the coffee table. "Like that open book over there."

Michael adjusts his coat. "Hey look, what happened on the couch just sort of caught me by surprise. That's all. I apologize if I insulted you or your friend. That really wasn't my intention." He extends his hand. "Still friends?"

She grabs his hand. "Of course, still friends."

She presses close to him.

He puts his arm around her waist, leans down, and kisses her on the lips, careful not to linger.

The kiss is nice, but the sharpness of their back-and-forth comments has dulled the passion.

Vickie steps back a step.

Michael steps back a step.

Vickie takes his arm and walks him to the front door.

"Michael, I really enjoyed dinner with you tonight," she says sweetly. "Thank you so much."

"The pleasure was mine. I'll call you soon."

"I would like that."

He opens the door and walks out into the hallway. He turns and looks back at her standing in the doorway. "I'm going to try to not think about you all night."

"Don't try too hard," she replies with a smile.

She watches him for a moment as he walks down the hallway towards the elevator. He gives her a final wave just before entering the elevator.

She waves back, and then gently closes the door.

CHAPTER IV

Jonathan is painting in his studio.
    His studio is a large, open space in the attic of the family's farmhouse. This is an artist's haven, cluttered with all the kinds of things one expects to see in such a place.
    Jonathan is also an accomplished sculptor, but there are no sculptures here. For that kind of messy work, Jonathan has created a workspace in a dilapidated storage building outside, next to the barn.
    The early morning sun is just beginning to illuminate the dormer windows. Jonathan likes to work with some, but not too much, natural sunlight. Too much natural light tends to obscure the subtle differences in the colors with which he works; thus he prefers painting in the early morning hours
    The rooster's crow is his cue to finish what he is doing and get ready for breakfast. The farm chores which loom beyond the windows are unforgiving and relentless.

    Jonathan has joined his family in sitting around the kitchen table.
    Out of necessity, breakfast is always a hearty meal. Farm work demands a high-calorie diet. But although they may eat like

workhorses, Jonathan and his siblings are as lean and hard as racehorses. Jonathan's father, Paul, has the physique of a fit man twenty-five years younger.

Jonathan reaches across the table for a thick slice of his mom's homemade bread and spreads butter on it. He takes a large bite out of it. He stops chewing only long enough to take a large gulp of milk. No one notices. Everyone else is busy taking their own bites and gulps, except his mother, Elizabeth. From across the table, she is watching him intently.

Jonathan looks up from his plate and sees his mother staring at him with a strange little smile on her face.

Jonathan puts his fork down on the plate and wipes his mouth with his napkin.

"Okay, Mom, what's on your mind?" he asks.

"What do you mean?" Elizabeth asks, feigning surprise.

Jonathan's father looks over at them, first at Elizabeth, then at Jonathan, and then he goes back to eating. The begging harvest mainly occupies Paul's mind this crisp autumn morning.

Jonathan wipes his hands with his napkin, which he then folds neatly and places on the table. "I know that look, Mom," he says as he leans back in his chair. "So tell me, what is it?"

Elizabeth folds her hands on her lap, and looks down. "Well, there is something I wanted to discuss with you."

A few moments pass by.

"Yes, Mom, go on," Jonathan urges.

"Well, it's just that, Sarah, the daughter of Robert and Margaret Stoltzfus is turning eighteen years next week. And they're having a gathering at their home for friends and family to celebrate this occasion. And they were hoping you would accept their invitation to attend, to join them in the celebration, at their home, with Sarah."

With a stern look on his face, Jonathan pushes his chair away from the table. He stands up and walks over to the wall where his straw hat is hanging on a hook. He removes his hat from the hook and walks around the table to where his mom is sitting.

She looks up at him.

He leans down and kisses her on her forehead. "Mom, you tell

Mr. and Mrs. Stoltzfus that I would be honored to join them in celebrating Sarah's eighteenth birthday."

He turns and looks over at his father, brothers, and sister. All of them are staring back at him, their mouths hanging open.

Jonathan puts on his hat, and smiles. "Let's get to work, guys. And I suggest you all better close your mouths before something crunchy flies in them."

Then he tips his hat and walks out the kitchen door. The screen door slams back against the frame.

Paul looks at Elizabeth, who now has a big grin on her face. She looks back at him and shrugs her shoulders. "Well, you've all got a lot of work to do today, and you're not going to get it done sitting here on your duffs."

She gets up and starts clearing the table. The boys scramble out of their chairs and out the kitchen door.

Paul stands up. His pants suspenders are hanging off his shoulders. His shirt tail is sticking out. He walks around the table to Elizabeth, and kisses her on the cheek. He pulls up his suspenders and tucks in his shirt.

"That was a mighty fine breakfast, love. Thank you," he says with a big smile, just before turning and walking out the back door.

The day of Sarah's birthday gathering is a perfect autumn Saturday. Wispy clouds of yellow and green accent bright, blue skies.

Jonathan is navigating a horse-drawn carriage along a narrow, country road.

An occasional car zips past him, kicking up dust as it roars by. Today, the obnoxious sound of their engines is not as annoying to him, most likely because he finds himself looking forward with unexpected anticipation to seeing Sarah for the first time in months.

As he slowly makes his way to her house, his mind starts meandering down memory lane, once again. His thoughts carry him back five years in time, to when he and Vickie were seventeen years of age.

Vickie is driving a small sedan with Jonathan sitting next to her. She has been unusually quiet, almost somber, since picking him up ten minutes ago.

Jonathan looks over at her. "Vickie, are you sure you're okay with this?"

"What are you talking about?"

"You know darn well what I'm talking about."

"Well, I might have an idea about what you're talking about," Vickie admits, with a glance over at him.

Jonathan narrows his eyes.

"Okay, okay," she sighs. "I might have a little touch of anxiety about our coming to this thing. But I'm not one bit afraid of doing it. In fact, it's long overdue. It's not like people haven't known about us for a long time. So what's the big deal?"

"I agree with you one hundred percent. It's no big deal," he replies.

Vickie manages a weak smile, which disappears quickly as she turns the car into an immense dirt parking lot.

In front of them, the annual town fair spreads out over a large, grassy field, like a giant picnic blanket filled with all the trimmings. In the distance, throngs of people mill about a maze of carnival rides, games, and food booths.

Vickie pulls the car into a parking space and turns off the engine.

She looks at Jonathan for a moment, and then reaches over and squeezes his hand. "I order you to have a good time."

Jonathan tips his hat. "Yes, ma'am."

Vickie knows that Amish folks enjoy picnics and fairs as much as anyone else. However, she also knows that they prefer to attend their own social gatherings, such as barn raisings and the like. It is no small show of affection for Jonathan to accompany her to this "English" fair.

She leans across the seat and kisses him on the cheek. "Thank you."

"Don't mention it," he replies. "Now, what're we waiting for? Let's go have some fun."

They step out of the car. Jonathan walks around the car, takes Vickie by the hand, and walks her through the entrance gate.

Once inside the fair grounds, they are immediately greeted, and even engaged in conversation by many of the local folks.

As it is, both Vickie and Jonathan are well known and greatly admired by the people in the Lancaster, Pennsylvania area. And the fact that one is Amish and the other is not does not seem to matter much to the great majority of the local folks.

The town's police chief, Bob Manning, is strolling around, shaking hands, making small talk. Though he appears relaxed and nonchalant, the truth is, his eyes are darting around like a hawk's, scanning everyone and everything around him. With a baton on one side of his waist and a walkie-talkie on the other side, the chief is here to make sure that everyone has a good time, and that no trouble occurs. The gun strapped to his ankle is discretely hidden under the leg of his trousers.

Chief Manning spots Vickie and Jonathan standing together just ahead of him. He walks up behind them and pats Vickie on the back. She turns around.

"Glad you two could make it."

"Thank you, Chief Manning," Vickie replies sweetly.

"Are you two kids having fun?" the chief asks, looking at Jonathan.

"Sir, we just got here. But yes, we aim to have ourselves a good time," Jonathan answers.

"Well, you two do just that, and that's an order. And if you need me for anything, be sure to let me know." Chief Manning then spots one of his deputies. "Hey, Jeff, hold up. I want to talk to you about something," he calls out. He gives Jonathan a pat on the shoulder before walking off.

Vickie and Jonathan look at each other. "Everyone is so nice," she says.

Jonathan nods in agreement.

Vickie hears live music coming from the open dance hall. "Let's dance," she says excitedly.

Before Jonathan can respond, she grabs him by the hand and

starts leading him towards the dance floor. Just before they reach the dance floor, a shrieking voice pierces the din of the crowd.

"Hey, farm boy, what're you doing here?"

Both Vickie and Jonathan turn to look in the direction of the obnoxious sounding voice.

A group of four college-age young men is walking towards them. The problem with this group is that they are not college boys. They are well-known local punks, and it is safe to assume that prison, not college, is the institution that looms in their immediate futures.

The leader of the group strides up to Jonathan. Jonathan stands his ground.

The lead thug looks back over his shoulder at his buddies. "Look, boys, we have a tough guy here."

Jonathan glares at him.

The tough guy starts taunting Jonathan. "What're you going to do, farm boy? Are you going to hit me, tough guy? Oh, I'm sorry. I forgot. You people are pacifists. You're not supposed to hit people, are you? Won't fight to defend your own country, will you?"

Then he brushes an imaginary something off Jonathan's shoulder. "If you ask me, that's just an excuse for being a bunch of yellow bellied cowards."

Until this point, Vickie has been standing shoulder to shoulder with Jonathan, just watching and listening. Well now, she has seen and heard enough. She steps in front of Jonathan and faces the tough guy.

"That's enough, Frankie!" she barks. "Leave him alone. He's not bothering you. Why are you bothering him? Or is it that you just can't help acting like a jerk all the time?"

Frankie takes a step back. "Hey look, Vickie, I'm just having some fun with your farm boy here. I don't mean any harm."

"Well then, stop insulting him and go about your business," Vickie demands.

Frankie smiles and starts backing up, with his hands raised in mock defense. "Yes, ma'am, whatever you say." He looks over at Jonathan. "Hey, Jonathan, no hard feelings, okay?"

Jonathan is having none of it, and he just keeps glaring at

him.

Vickie grabs Jonathan by the arm and pulls him away. "Come on, Jonathan. Let's go. I want that dance now."

She leads him to the center of the dance floor and starts dancing. "Don't let that moron ruin your day, Jonathan. Come on now, twinkle toes, I've seen you dance."

Jonathan cracks a smile.

They start dancing.

Minutes later, Frankie walks up behind Jonathan and taps him on the shoulder. Jonathan turns around.

"Mind if I cut in, partner?" Frankie asks politely.

Jonathan looks at Vickie.

"It's okay, Jonathan," she says.

Jonathan tips his hat to Vickie and starts walking off the dance floor, slowly making his way through the crowd.

Vickie watches Jonathan for a moment, and then she turns to Frankie.

Frankie is now looking at Vickie with a devilish smile on his face. "You don't have to worry, Vickie. I'm not gonna bite you. I just wanna dance with the prettiest girl in town."

"That's fine, Frankie, just as long as you behave yourself," Vickie warns him.

"I promise...scout's honor, stick a needle in my eye, or whatever," Frankie says, his hand in the air like he is being sworn in by a judge in a court of law.

Vickie muses to herself. "Frankie, I'm sure you're going to meet many judges, in many courtrooms, before your days are over."

They are dancing nicely, when suddenly, the band transitions into a slow song.

Vickie stops and looks at Frankie. "Oh, no, no, this wasn't part of the deal," she protests.

"If you just give me a chance, doll face, you'll see that I'm not such a bad guy," he pleads.

"Okay, Frankie, but just this one dance. And not too close," she says as she moves back a step, puts her left hand on his right shoulder, and holds up her right hand for him to take.

Frankie looks at her and laughs. "You must be kidding," he says as he grabs her around the waist, and pulls her close. "Don't worry, Vickie. Relax. I'll be a good boy."

Not one bit does Vickie like having Frankie's arm around her waist, but because she wants to defuse the combustible situation between Jonathan and Frankie, she decides not to push him away.

Frankie's face is so close to hers that she can smell his breath.

She looks around for Jonathan.

"Don't worry about him, Vickie. He's probably hitched a ride back home to the farm," Frankie says, sarcastically.

Frankie tightens his grip around Vickie's waist and presses his body into hers.

Vickie immediately protests. "Frankie, not so tight. I don't like it!"

"Oh, hell, baby. You know you like being held by a real man."

She tries to wrestle out of his arms. "I said, let go of me, Frankie," she demands.

Frankie ignores her and tightens his arms around her waist.

"Get the hell off of me," Vickie shouts as she tries to push him back off of her.

Finally, when that fails, she rears back, in desperation, and slaps Frankie across the face.

Her small hand must pack quite a wallop, because Frankie instantly drops his arms from around her waist and stumbles backwards, grabbing at his cheek.

Shocked at how hard she slapped Frankie, Vickie stands there, with her hands covering her mouth. "Frankie, I'm so sorry. I didn't mean to hit you that hard."

More stunned than hurt, Frankie takes a moment to gather himself, while gingerly patting his now-burning cheek. Then he slowly turns his attention to Vickie, his eyes glaring at her.

Seeing the menace in his eyes, Vickie takes a defensive step backwards.

"You bitch! Nobody slaps me like that!" he snarls, his teeth bared like a crazed dog.

Vickie turns to get away from him, but with a quick move, he lunges at her, grabs her long hair, and yanks her back.

Holding her tightly by her hair and forcing her head back, Frankie raises his fist to strike her, but just as his fist begins to move forward, a hand reaches from behind and grabs his wrist, stopping it dead in midair.

"What the...?" Frankie utters, as he turns his head, and sees Jonathan standing behind him.

Jonathan's eyes are on fire.

Before Frankie can react, Jonathan quickly grips Frankie's shoulder with his other hand, and digs his powerful fingers into Frankie's trapezius muscle, crushing into its tissue with the power of a steel vice.

Instantly Frankie releases Vickie's hair and drops to his knees.

About this time, Frankie's three buddies spot him through the crowd, writhing and moaning on the ground, with Jonathan standing over him, still holding Frankie's wrist in a bone-crushing grip with one hand, and mangling the soft tissues of his shoulder with the other hand.

"Get him," one of them shouts out, as they start charging towards Jonathan.

Jonathan looks up and sees them coming. He lets go of Frankie, tossing him aside like a rag doll, and turns towards the charging thugs, his huge fists clenched and ready to rain hell down on these unsuspecting punks. Jonathan's sense of Amish pacifism is clearly not applying to those who would threaten or harm someone he loves, like Vickie.

Without realizing it, the three young men are hurdling themselves towards imminent doom at the hands of an enraged Jonathan, when suddenly, a police baton whips through the air and cracks against the lead guy's shin bone. The guy drops like a sack of Idaho potatoes thrown off the back of a truck.

Like his buddy, Frankie, he, too, is now on the ground writhing and moaning.

Chief Manning steps across him, straddling the poor fellow's chest.

The other two guys see Chief Manning waiting for them, his baton at the ready, cocked at his side, and they wisely stop dead in their tracks.

The chief shouts out a warning. "Listen up, boys. I'm going to tell you one time, and one time only: you all better turn around right now, and get on out of here, before one or both of you gets what he just got." He points his baton at the guy lying between his legs. Then he motions his baton at the two guys on the ground, both still rocking and whimpering. "And take your two friends with you."

"Yes, sir," one of them says.

Chief Manning now walks over to where Frankie still sits, slumped on his knees, his head hanging down. His puts the tip of his baton under Frankie's chin and lifts his head up. He leans down really close to Frankie and whispers into his ear so that no one else can hear what he is saying.

"Listen up, boy. If I catch you causing trouble in my town again, you may find yourself accidentally falling into someone's hog pen at feeding time. And we'll make sure those hogs haven't been fed in days. You get my meaning, boy?"

Frankie barely has the strength to nod yes.

Chief Manning straightens up and motions for Frankie's friends to come over. They scramble over to Frankie and the other guy and help them to their feet. The four deviants stumble away.

Chief Manning keeps his eyes on them until they disappear through the exit gate, and then he turns to Vickie. "Are you okay, young lady? It looked like that woman-beater had a pretty tight grip on your hair."

"I'm okay, Chief Manning, thank you," Vickie replies.

The chief then turns to Jonathan. "I've got to tell you, son, you've got a grip like a steel vice. I must say I'm mighty impressed. Now I want you to get this nonsense out of your mind. I can assure you that it's over. You and Vickie go on and have a good time now."

Jonathan tips his hat. "Thank you, sir."

Vickie walks up to the chief and takes his hand in hers. "Thank you again for your help, Chief Manning."

"Well, you're welcome. But I must tell you, those four boys are the ones who should be thanking me," the chief replies. "I was saving them from Jonathan, not the other way around. Now, I want to see you two kids back out on that dance floor straight away. And I mean it."

Chief Manning motions to the band. "Come on, boys; let's fire up that music again."

The band starts up.

Jonathan and Vickie stand in front of each other. Vickie reaches out with her hands. Jonathan takes them. Vickie looks up at him. He looks down at her. A smile begins to form on his face.

"Well, what do you know? I believe my farm boy is smiling again," Vickie says. "But one thing is for certain, Jonathan Schaeffer, you are going to teach me that vice-grip-on-the-shoulder-pressure-point thing as soon as possible." And she is not joking.

The roar of a passing pickup truck awakens Jonathan from his daytime reverie.

As he draws closer to Sarah's farmhouse in the distance, he sees that other carriages are feeding into the main road from smaller roads.

When he moves up alongside one of these merging buggies, he sees that the driver is a young man by the name of Peter Lapp. Peter lives on a neighboring farm with his family. Though Jonathan does not know Peter well, he has spoken to him a few times at other social gatherings.

Peter and his family are known to be strict traditionalists. Jonathan is on the opposite end of the Amish cultural and religious spectrum from them. Jonathan's friendship with the "English" girl is common knowledge among the Amish of Lancaster County. And Jonathan is fully aware that Peter and his family are far too conservative to ever approve of such a relationship.

Jonathan pulls up alongside Peter and glances over at him. Peter looks over at him and smiles tepidly. Jonathan tips his hat and looks back to the road. Peter gives his horse a tap with the reins. His carriage quickly jumps ahead of Jonathan's. Jonathan fights the urge to challenge him, and he lets him pull away.

Moments later, Peter swings his carriage into the driveway of the farmhouse, with Jonathan right on his heels.

A dozen buggies are already parked along both sides of the long, dirt driveway. Except for their swatting tails, the carriage horses are standing as still as statues.

Jonathan swerves his buggy to the side of the driveway and brings it to a stop. He leans over and engages the parking brake.

From where he is sitting in his buggy, he glances up at the modest farmhouse and sees a young woman looking down at him through a second-floor window. Her long, strawberry-blond hair crowns a pleasantly rounded face. Her large, blue eyes are focused on him like laser beams. He smiles at her and tips his hat. She smiles back at him, and then quickly disappears from the window. "I may be in trouble," he says to himself as his gaze lingers on the window.

He gathers himself, takes a deep breath, and climbs down from the buggy. He slowly walks up the front porch steps, doing his best to not look overly anxious. Just as he raises his hand to knock on the front door, it opens.

Sarah's father, Isaac Stoltzfus, is standing in the doorway. "Good day, Jonathan," he says pleasantly. "How are you today?"

Jonathan removes his hat. "I'm fine, sir. Thank you."

"I'm glad you could make it. Come on in. We'll be eating soon, so I hope you brought your appetite."

Jonathan walks into the small foyer. "Yes, sir. I sure am hungry."

"Why don't you head out to the backyard? I think you'll find some folks out there that you know."

"I believe I'll do that. Thank you, sir," Jonathan says with a nod of his head.

Just as soon as Jonathan turns and starting walking away, Mr. Stoltzfus loses his smile. He narrows his eyes and watches Jonathan until he disappears through the rear doorway.

The backyard is bustling with Amish folks of all ages. The older men are sitting together in clusters, chatting quietly, and sipping cold lemonade and apple cider. Young men and women are scattered about, flirting with one another. And of course, the children are running about, making as much noise as they can get away with.

Several young men spot Jonathan just as soon as he walks out the back door. One of them rushes over to him. "Jonathan, it's good to see you," he says excitedly, extending his hand. "I wasn't sure you were coming."

Jonathan grabs his hand, and gives it a firm shake. "It's good to see you, too, Seth."

Seth pats him on the back. "It's been too long, my friend. We've missed you at the other gatherings. It makes some of us wonder if you've been trying to avoid us."

"Seth, I haven't been trying to avoid anyone. I just haven't felt very sociable lately,"

Seth grabs Jonathan by the arm and leads him a few yards away from the others. "Look, Jonathan, I know what's been going on with you. I know this is about the 'English' girl."

Jonathan tries to respond, but Seth cuts him off. "Don't deny it, my friend. I've known you my whole life."

Jonathan smiles and puts his arm around Seth's shoulder. "Look, Seth, I'm not going to lie to you. You're right about Vickie. But I will tell you this; I've been in a lot better state of mind lately. I'm glad to be here. And I'm glad to see you."

"And I'm glad to see you," Seth quickly answers back.

He and Jonathan give each other a quick hug and a slap on the back.

"Come with me," Seth says, again taking Jonathan by the arm. "I want to introduce you to some people."

The two young men walk over to a small group standing a few yards away. This group has been quietly talking among themselves while managing to steal glances over at Jonathan and Seth. Jonathan introduces himself to each one. Although he may not know them, one thing is certain, they all know him or have heard about him.

The girls shake his hand nervously, blushing noticeably. He pretends not to notice.

Their group grows larger as others begin gravitating towards them. Over the years, the young "English" ladies in the area have mostly fantasized about Jonathan, without any real hope of ever being with him. Vickie was the exception. She stole his heart years ago. And though the "English" girls accepted their fate, the young, eligible Amish ladies have always looked at Vickie as a sort of foreign usurper, all the while considering themselves to be the rightful contenders for his hand in marriage. Now several of these same young women are closing in around Jonathan, vying for his attention, and spinning their webs.

Just as the drama begins to unfold, Sarah appears on the back porch. Jonathan sees her, and stops talking in mid-sentence.

There is no mistaking the object of her interest. She looks at Jonathan as if he is the only person in the backyard.

His heart skips a beat. That Sarah has transformed from the awkward little girl he once knew into a woman of extraordinary beauty hits him like a thump on the chest. Her long, strawberry-blond hair is now pulled back into a tight bun, hidden under a black bonnet. The black bonnet signifies to all young, eligible, Amish men that she is now ready and available for courtship and marriage.

Jonathan quickly searches his short-term memory-bank for the image of Sarah standing at the second floor window with her long hair cascading down over her shoulders, and her dark blue eyes burning their imprints on his retinas. When he finds that image, he takes a deep breath, removes his hat, and begins walking towards her. To him, in the distance, Sarah appears sharply defined by a surrounding glow, while everything and everyone else around her appears blurred; out of focus. It is taking all of his concentration to not walk like he has two left feet.

All around them, there is silence, except for the squeals of the little ones playing in the background. All are watching them, trying not to stare. All are listening; straining to hear.

Jonathan reaches Sarah and extends his hand. "It's nice to see you again, Sarah."

Sarah takes his hand and gives it a firm shake. "It's nice to see you, too, Jonathan," she replies. "Thank you for coming today."

"Thank you for inviting me."

"I must say that I had my doubts that you would be here today,"

Sarah says.

"Why?" Jonathan asks.

"You know why, Jonathan."

Jonathan looks down. "Yes, I do know why."

"Well, anyway, I'm very happy you're here," Sarah says, letting him off the hook. "We're going to start the dancing soon, and I will be expecting a dance with you."

"It will be my pleasure."

Sarah smiles, and then turns and walks back into the house.

Jonathan watches her until she disappears through the doorway.

When he turns around, Peter Lapp is standing right in front of him.

"How's your 'English' girlfriend?" Peter asks, his tone sarcastic, his hands in his hip pockets.

Jonathan slips his hands into his pockets. "Normally, Peter, I would tell you in no uncertain terms to mind your own business. But because I'm in a good mood today, I will answer your question."

He takes a step towards Peter. Peter pulls his hands out of his pockets and takes a step backwards.

"Relax, Peter," Jonathan says calmly. "The answer to your question is that I don't know, because I haven't talked to her in a long while. But if you hear anything worthwhile, be sure to let me know."

Jonathan then turns and walks away.

A few hours later, a group of laughing and bantering young men and women is walking down a dirt path towards a large barn. Their outlines are silhouetted against the setting sun. In the twilight of the dusk, their long shadows dance eerily against the wooden walls on the outside of the hulking barn.

On the inside, the sturdy old barn is resonating with music, and jammed with frenetically dancing young Amish folk.

Their shirts soaked with sweat, the young men swing their partners around and around. The long hair and skirts of the young ladies fly out with every turn, and every spin. The mating dance of the young Amish is in full swing. And Jonathan and Sarah are right in the middle of the undulating dance floor.

His face glistening with sweat, Jonathan leans in close to Sarah's ear. "Let's get some fresh air."

Sarah nods okay.

Jonathan takes her hand. "Do you want something to drink?" he asks.

"Yes, that would be nice. It's very hot in here," Sarah replies, fanning herself with her hand.

"Wait here. I'll be right back."

A few minutes later, Jonathan is making his way back towards Sarah with a paper cup of lemonade in each hand, when he sees her through the crowd. She is surrounded by a group of young men. They are all chatting easily with one another, like the long-time friends that they are. Sarah is in the middle of the group, clearly enjoying their attention. Her long hair covers her shoulders and cascades down to the middle of her back.

Sarah turns and fixes her piercing eyes on Jonathan as he moves slowly through the dense crowd towards her. By the time he reaches Sarah, the men around her have dissolved away. They know. They saw the way she looked at Jonathan.

He stands in front of her for a few moments, speechless.

"Is one of those for me?" Sarah asks.

He just stares at her, not answering.

"Jonathan, is one of those for me?" she again asks, pointing to the cup in his right hand.

Hearing his name seems to shake him out of his trance. "Oh, yes. I'm sorry. This is for you," he answers, handing her the cup of lemonade.

"It feels so nice and cold," she says, smiling, as she takes a long sip from the cup.

"It's really warm in here," she observes, as she gathers up her long, golden hair in one hand, lifts it high over her head, and lets it fall back over her shoulders. Not yet finished, she leans back and slowly runs her hand sensuously through her hair. When she is finally finished throwing her hair around, she looks at Jonathan and smiles innocently, as if she has no clue that he is precariously close to getting sucked into the vortex of her swirling hair.

Jonathan takes her hand. "Let's get out of here."

He leads her out of the barn and into the night.

The fresh air moistens their dry throats. A light breeze cools their flushed skin.

Later that night, Jonathan is lying on his bed, stretched out on his back. The moonlight is stealing in through the window and illuminating one side of his face. The other side is hidden in the shadows. His head is resting on a pillow. His hands lay folded on his chest.

Glowing in the moon's light, his eyes appear to turn on and off with each blink of his eyelids. His eyelids are growing heavy. His breathing speeds up for a few seconds, and then slows down. A deep inspiration heralds sweet sleep, if not-so-sweet dreams.

Jonathan is steering a horse-driven harvester through a freshly cut field of hay. He is headed back to the barn as the long work day draws to an end. A warm breeze caresses his face. The late afternoon day is unusually humid. Clusters of thick, gray clouds hang ominously low in the sky. The sun appears to be floating just above the horizon.

Jonathan turns and looks over to a narrow dirt road that runs alongside the field. Standing in the distance is a young, Amish woman. Her appearance intrigues him, as she is not wearing the white bonnet typical of Amish women. Instead, a black scarf covers her hair and hides her face.

He pulls back hard on the reins to stop the horses. He ties the reins to the brake handle, jumps down off the machine, and starts walking towards the woman. The woman is standing as still as a statue in a museum. Her head is down; her face hidden from his view.

"Sarah?" Jonathan calls out.

She does not answer.

He cups his hands around his mouth. "Sarah, is that you?" he again calls out. Again, there is no response.

Suddenly, the sky is turning dark, as if someone is drawing a shade down over the sun. Jonathan looks up and sees thick black clouds rolling across the sky. He looks back in the direction of the woman.

Without warning, she suddenly takes off running down the dirt road.

"Sarah, stop. Come back," he yells out. "It's going to…"

Suddenly, a massive bolt of lightening explodes from the sky, stabbing through the clouds like a giant dagger. Seconds after the lightening strike, its jagged wound, burned into the clouds, still glows against the darkened sky.

Then a rolling clap of thunder reverberates across the countryside, just as a torrent of rain bursts from the pregnant clouds above. In an instant, Jonathan is drenched, as if he just walked under a waterfall. The warmth of the water against his skin both startles and pleases him.

Though Jonathan can barely see through the dense sheets of water cascading from the sky, he keeps looking for the woman. He starts running down the dirt road, which by now has been turned into a river of mud by the raging downpour. He calls out her name. "Sarah! Sarah!" But his voice is drowned out by the din of the colliding elements.

After staggering another twenty yards, he stops in the middle of the road and wipes his eyes with both hands. From out of nowhere, the woman appears in front of him. Her head is turned away. The scarf is gone, ripped away from her head and devoured by the fierce rain. Her long hair hangs down all around her, covering her face.

Jonathan stumbles to within a few feet of the woman. "Sarah, are you okay?" he stammers, barely able to breathe through the water pouring into his nose and mouth.

The woman does not answer.

He reaches towards her with a trembling hand and lifts her hair away from her face. He wipes the water from his eyes and stares into her face.

"Vickie?"

Vickie just stares back at him with hollow eyes.

Stunned, Jonathan reaches out to touch her face. "Vickie,

what are you...?" he starts to ask. But before he can finish his sentence, she again disappears within the blinding glow of another lightening bolt.

Moments later, Jonathan is lying on his back in a muddy quagmire. His eyelids are flickering in that twilight realm of semi-consciousness, just before one awakens. And then his eyes open, and he is looking up at wispy white clouds floating gracefully in a bright, azure sky.

When he tries to sit up, his hands sink into soft, wet mud, and he falls back awkwardly. With the second attempt, he succeeds in getting up on his feet in the slippery mud without falling. Once on his feet, he starts looking all around frantically, like a child lost in a forest.

"Where is she?" he asks out loud to no one; to anyone.

"I'm here, Jonathan," is a soft reply from behind.

He turns around.

Vickie is standing in front of him, wearing a traditional Amish wedding dress, pristine and white. Her hair is neatly tucked under a black bonnet.

She places her hand over her heart. "I'm right here, Jonathan." Her light brown eyes are glowing. "No other woman will ever love you the way I love you." She reaches her hand towards him. "Come to me now, my love."

He takes a step forward and reaches for her hand.

Jonathan wakes up in a warm sweat.

He sits up and swings his legs over the edge of the bed.

"Now I'm having dreams about Vickie telling me to 'come to me now, my love'. What else is next?" he asks himself out loud, shaking his head.

Jonathan cradles his head in his hands, his shoulders slumped. His neck muscles are as taut as piano strings. He gets up and walks slowly to the bathroom, moving stiffly, like an old man.

The early morning sunlight colors his room a hazy gray. It is that time of the morning when one can just begin to make out forms in the darkness; when a man can walk around free of his own shadow.

Jonathan turns on the sink faucet, and without waiting for the water to run warm, cups his hands under the stream and splashes ice-cold water on his face.

As water drips from his chin, he studies his reflection in the mirror. He barely recognizes his own face. He might as well be looking at a stranger inside the mirror.

A short time later, he steps lightly down the stairs, not wanting to awaken anyone.

He turns into the kitchen and sees his mother bent over the stove, adjusting the flame under the coffee pot.

"Are you ready for a cup of coffee?" she asks without turning around.

Jonathan takes his hat off. "That sounds real good, Mom." He walks over to her and kisses her on the cheek. "I wanted to get an early start on buying some supplies in town. I can't stand the rush-hour traffic."

"I heard you up early this morning," Elizabeth says, turning around and facing him.

Jonathan slides a chair out from under the table and sits down. "I've been having some trouble sleeping lately, so I figured I might as well make use of my time. It's a whole lot better than just lying in bed watching the spiders on the ceiling spinning their webs."

Elizabeth turns back to the stove and pours the hot coffee into a cup. She walks over and hands the cup to Jonathan. He carefully sips the hot brew. For a few moments, he stares at the steam curling up from the coffee cup. When he looks up, his mother is still looking at him.

"Okay, Mom, I'll tell you what's bothering me," he says. "It's not that complicated. Actually, it's pretty simple. I just have a way of making it complicated." He looks up at her, waiting for a response.

She lets him keep talking.

"You know how much the family means to me," he continues. "You know how much I appreciate our life here on the farm. And yet I keep on believing that there is something more for me out there." He points his finger in the air. "I have to believe the good

Lord put me on this earth for something more. Of course, I want to be a husband and a father someday. But for some reason, and I don't know why, I believe that I'm meant to be more than a farmer. There are lots of farmers. Now don't get me wrong, Mom, I respect farm life. But in my heart, I believe there is something else I'm supposed to be doing, and what that is, I can't do it here. And that's the problem, Mom. To do what I feel I need to do, I would have to leave you guys. And I don't know if I can do that."

Tears start to well up in his mother's eyes.

When Jonathan sees this, he jumps up from the chair and walks over to her. "Mom, you don't have to cry. When I say leave my family, I mean leave the Amish ways. I don't mean leaving you and Dad and the kids. I would always be around, so much so you'll be yawning and saying how it's past your bedtime and shooing me out the door."

Elizabeth wipes her nose with the tissue. "I would never do that."

"You may have to do that, just to get rid of me."

Elizabeth looks at him. "What about Sarah?"

"I like Sarah very much, but she represents something that I'm not sure I'm ready to commit to for the rest of my life."

Jonathan walks across the kitchen to where his hat hangs on the wall and removes it from the hook. He starts fingering the brim of the hat and looking at his mother. For a long while, this goes on.

"What is it, Jonathan?" she finally asks.

Jonathan puts his hat back on its hook, walks over to the table and sits back down. He leans over the table. "You know, mother, you and Vickie are a lot alike. She's a talented singer and songwriter. And you are a talented fashion designer."

"What are you talking about?" she whispers loudly.

"You know exactly what I'm talking about, Mother. The fact is you could have started your own fashion label if you had wanted to. You were that good. Maybe you should have pursued your dreams."

"What do you know about my dreams? Elizabeth asks indignantly.

Jonathan leans back in his chair. "When I was little, I used to sneak into your room and get into things. One day, I found a notebook of your drawings. They were amazing. Back then, you always seemed to have a gleam in your eyes, like you were always excited about something. I haven't seen that twinkle in your eyes for a long time. It's like you just gave up on your dreams, Mom. And when you just give up on something so important…well, every time that I get up, get dressed in these clothes, and go outside to do whatever this farm demands me to do, a little bit more of me dies each day."

Jonathan studies his mother's face for a few moments. "I can't read your thoughts, Mom."

Elizabeth turns, walks over to the stove, and stands with her back to him for a few moments. Then, as if she has found the right words, she whirls around and looks him straight in the eyes.

"When I lay my eyes on you and the others at the start of every new day, my heart jumps out of my chest. You say I've lost that gleam in my eyes, but what you don't see is the joy in my heart and the comfort in my soul that I feel whenever I sit down at the table with my family. For me now, you and the others are my life. And there is no career success; no amount of fame and fortune that could ever equal the happiness that I feel in my heart whenever I hear your footsteps and those of the others coming down those stairs in the morning. Yes, you're probably right when you say that I would have loved a career in fashion design. But I would never trade my family and the life that I have now for anything. I would rather die."

Jonathan gets up from the table and walks over to his mother. He takes her hands in his. "I know, Mom. I expected you to say those things. But unlike you, I don't know what I want. I'm at that bend in the river. I want to be an artist, but I want to be here with my family everyday; to see and hear you guys everyday, and not just when I come home for visits that are always over too soon."

"Jonathan, if you go off to New York, or wherever, to be an artist, to be with Vickie, or whomever, you will not lose us. And even when you're not physically here with us, we will always be right here," she says as she places her hand over his heart.

"But the truth is, I don't know if I'm strong enough to go out there on my own, without you guys," he confesses as he covers her hand with his.

"You're strong enough, Jonathan. I have no doubt that you can do whatever you want to do. But don't think for a moment that we won't continue to be a large part of your life, and your children's lives; whether you're here or there, it doesn't matter, not one bit. But you know darn well that, in the end, you have to follow your heart, because no matter what you decide to do in life, if your heart is not in it, you will never truly be happy. And you'll always be asking yourself, 'What if...?'"

Jonathan lets go of her hand, leans back against the counter, and looks down at the floor.

Elizabeth understands too well the conflict roiling inside her oldest son.

"Think about what I've said, Jonathan," she says. "Every bit of it is true. Anyway, you needn't make any decisions right now. Give it time. The decision will come to you when the time is right. And when it does, I am confident that you will do what is the right thing for you. Just believe in yourself. And remember, and never forget, that no matter what that decision is, you will always be my son, and I will always be your mother, and you will always be a big part of this family. And nothing can ever change that."

Elizabeth lifts Jonathan's chin and looks into his eyes.

"Okay? Did you hear me?" she asks.

"Yes, Mother. I heard every word."

He kisses her on the cheek, puts on his hat, and walks over to the back door. Just before opening the door, he turns.

"Thanks, Mom. I'll be back for breakfast."

He then tips his hat and walks out the door, gently closing the screen door behind him.

CHAPTER V

Jonathan steers his buggy around a corner and swings it into the parking lot of Milligan's Hardware Supplies. He deftly maneuvers the horse and carriage between two parked cars, and then pulls back hard on the reins. "Whoa, boy," he barks.

The horse stops.

"Good boy," he says as he pulls back on the handbrake, locking it into place.

He climbs down from the buggy and strides across the parking lot to the entrance of the store. Just before entering the store, something catches his eye. He turns and walks over to a rack carrying a stack of the local newspaper. He picks up one of the papers and stares at the headlines. It reads in bold letters, "LOCAL GIRL RETURNS TO PERFORM IN BENEFIT PERFORMANCE."

The article below the headline begins, "Lancaster native and now international singing star, Victoria Shaheen, will be appearing this Saturday at the New American Music Theater in a benefit performance to raise money for the FEED THE WORLD organization."

Jonathan smiles and puts the newspaper back on the stack. When he turns to walk into the store, he almost bumps into a man standing behind him.

"Excuse me...Mr. Shaheen," Jonathan stammers. The man standing in front of him is Vickie's father, Philip Shaheen.

A man in his early fifties, Philip Shaheen is a lean and handsome man of impeccable grooming. Philip was born in Philadelphia to immigrant parents who became naturalized citizens of the United States.

Philip's father was from Beirut, Lebanon; his mother from Paris. They met while studying at the University of Paris. Sadly, both have since passed away. Neither one of them lived long enough to see their granddaughter, Vickie, become an international singing star.

Philip Shaheen was raised a Roman Catholic, like both of his parents. But now, the only time he sees the inside of a church is for funerals or marriages.

And also like his parents, he met his wife, Vickie's mother, Veronica, at a university. They fell in love while both were attending Penn State University. Philip received his degree in economics. Veronica's degree was in music, a field in which she remains very busy as a private piano teacher and a much-sought-after accompanist. Needless to say, Vickie's musicianship comes from her mother's genes.

Philip has been very successful in the computer consulting business. And to say the least, he has invested his money wisely. Financially, the Shaheen family is a lot more than well-off. But because the family chooses to live modestly, only their closest friends and relatives are privy to their affluence. An intensely private man, Philip prefers it this way.

As for his now-famous daughter, Victoria, he is more proud of her having graduated with a Bachelor of Fine Arts degree from the Juilliard School of Music than for her wealth and success as a professional singer. Education is and will always be of paramount importance in the Shaheen family.

On the surface, Philip appears stern and imposing. But behind his rough veneer is a warm and generous man. Only his family and close friends know his true nature. He rarely smiles in public. People outside his small social circle are never sure what to expect from him, and so they usually keep their distance. He likes it that way. Small talk does not interest him.

Though at first startled to see Vickie's father, Jonathan quickly pulls himself together.

"Mr. Shaheen…Hello. It's been awhile. How are you, sir?"

"I'm fine, Jonathan. Thanks for asking. And how are you and your family?"

"We're all doing well. Thank you."

"That's good to hear."

"You're up mighty early this morning, sir," Jonathan notes.

"I wanted to get some chores done this morning before I head to the airport for an overnight business trip," Philip explains.

"You and I had the same notion this morning," Jonathan observes in an upbeat tone.

They look at each other during an awkward moment of silence.

Philip breaks the silence. "Well, Jonathan, you know, I'm glad we bumped into each other. It gives me a chance to tell you that I have it on very good information that Victoria would be very pleased if you could be there this Saturday," he says, pointing to the headlines on the newspaper.

Jonathan responds without hesitation. "Mr. Shaheen, I wouldn't want to be any place else that day. Yes, sir, I will be there Saturday."

Philip smiles and extends his hand. "Thank you, Jonathan. She will be very excited to hear that."

Jonathan grabs his hand and shakes it. "Thank you, Mr. Shaheen. Thank you very much."

Philip gives Jonathan a pat on the shoulder. "It was good to see you again, Jonathan. And don't be a stranger."

"It was good to see you, too, sir. And I won't."

Philip nods his head and smiles before turning and getting into his car.

Jonathan watches him drive off. "That's the first time I've ever seen him smile," he says out loud to himself.

While watching Philip drive away, Jonathan reaches for the store's front door. The young ladies watching him through the windows from inside the store scatter like a flock of birds.

Back at home an hour later, Jonathan opens the back door to the kitchen. His mother is putting the finishing touches on breakfast.

He walks over to the kitchen table, pulls out a chair, and sits down.

"Okay, Mom, did you know about Vickie coming to town next week?"

"Oh, I might have heard a rumor," she says coyly as she flips over a pancake, cooking on the grill.

"Were you planning to tell me?"

Without saying a word, Jonathan's mother walks over to a small desk in the corner of the kitchen, opens a drawer, and takes out a brightly colored, single-page pamphlet. She walks over to Jonathan and hands it to him.

He reads the bold headlines on the flier, announcing next week's benefit concert with Vickie, the premier performer.

"Where did you get this, Mom?"

"Mr. Shaheen dropped it off here this morning."

"Mr. Shaheen? Mom, you won't believe who I ran into at Miligan's."

"I know, Jonathan. I sent him there to find you," his mother says as she places a platter of pancakes in the middle of the table.

"I should have known it was too much of a coincidence," Jonathan says, slapping his thigh with his hand.

"It seems to me that most coincidences that happen in life are of an unimportant nature," his mother replies, a wry smile on her face.

"You're probably right about that, too, Mom. Anyway, do you know what he said to me? He actually asked me to go to Vickie's benefit concert, that she would be very pleased if I would be there. Of course I said that I was going. He then smiles…the first time I've ever seen him smile. He then shakes my hand. And so there I am, shaking his hand, up and down, like some sort of wind-up toy."

He pauses to take a breath.

Elizabeth carries a bowl of strawberries over to the table.

Jonathan starts tapping his boot nervously on the floor. "The feelings I had while reading in the local paper about her returning home; I haven't felt like that in a long time. It sure stirred up a lot of things inside me, I'll tell you that. Yes, I am going. It'll be the hardest thing I've ever done, and the easiest; if you know what I mean."

"I know exactly what you mean," Elizabeth replies. "Now hurry and get washed up. And tell the others that breakfast is ready."

"Yes, ma'am."

Jonathan jumps up from his chair and gives his mom a kiss on the forehead. He then bounds up the stairs, two steps at a time.

CHAPTER VI

Back in New York City, on the eve of the benefit concert, Vickie is rushing around in her Upper West Side apartment. A large suitcase lies open on her bed.

The phone rings. She frowns before picking up a portable phone sitting on the night stand.

"Hello," she answers, not too pleasantly.

Her frown quickly melts into a smile. "Oh, hi, Mom. I'm sorry. I thought you were someone else."

Vickie pauses. "Oh, don't worry. It doesn't matter." Another pause. "I can't wait to see all of you, too. I really miss you guys."

She puts the phone under her chin and starts folding a blouse. "Yes, I'm packing now. I never know what to bring, so I'm pretty much bringing everything. You know that I need a professional packer."

Vickie stops folding and sighs deeply. "No, Mom, we're going to drive down. Don't worry, Tony is an excellent driver. And I'm the worst backseat driver. I know that I annoy him terribly. But I just don't like speeding and cutting in and out of lanes. He knows how I am, and is very good about not doing those things."

Vickie is bending over to place the blouse into the suitcase when she suddenly straightens up, like she just got slapped on her backside. "How do you know he's going to be there? Are you sure?" Her voice is getting higher with each question. "Daddy did that?"

Feeling her knees getting weak, she looks for somewhere to sit down. She makes it over to the chaise longue and collapses onto it. She starts talking like an out-of-breath teenage girl who just got asked to the prom by the boy she hoped and prayed would ask her, but without truly believing it would ever happen.

"Mom, I know that in the back of my mind I hoped that somehow he would be there, smiling at me from the front row, or that he would come backstage to my dressing room, and that we would grab me and lift me up in his arms and say how much he loved me and would never leave me again. But I wouldn't let myself believe that this could actually happen. No matter what you might think, I am not coming home to do this concert so that I could see him and somehow win him back. It really never occurred to me that he might actually be there. Well, that's not exactly the truth. If I believed that happy endings occur only in romantic comedy movies, or in romance novels written for teenage girls, then I would be a lot more cynical than I am. But I'm not going to get crazy about this."

She holds out her hand. "Mom, my hand is shaking."

She stops talking long enough to take a breath and listen to her mom on the other line.

"I know, Mom. I'm not going to get my hopes too high," she replies to her mother.

Vickie jumps up and starts pacing around the room. "I'm fine. I'm calm. I'm a grown woman, fully in control of my emotions. Mom, I am so not in control right now. Listen, let me call you back. I've got to go to the bathroom and scream my head off. I love you, too. Talk to you soon."

Vickie clicks the phone off and throws it onto the couch. She walks over to the bed, turns around, and collapses onto it.

The next day, Vickie's vehicle is traveling through the gently rolling hills of the Pennsylvania farm country. She has been gone from her hometown for only a few years, but to her, it seems like a lifetime.

As familiar sites start whizzing past the car, she begins to feel a tingling sensation at the base of her neck. Her anxiety level is rising like the mercury of an old-fashioned thermometer. Waves of nausea begin rolling back and forth in her gut like barrels of rum on the deck of an Elizabethan dreadnought sailing in rough seas.

As she gazes out the backseat window, her thoughts are running an obstacle course of questions. What if he really shows up? What if he doesn't? What if he's cold and distant? How should I react? What should I say? How will I sing? How will I survive this nerve-racking, emotional rollercoaster?

But a different feeling is starting to well up inside of her. Slowly but surely, a growing excitement is starting to elbow aside the anxiety. She recognizes and welcomes this familiar emotion. It is the same feeling she has when she is standing in the wings of the stage, just before a performance.

The sun is low in the cloudless sky. The shadows of farmhouses, silos, and barns creep along the rolling farmland. A parade of lights and colors reflects across her window; her face barely visible behind the crazily dancing forms.

The car pulls up to the front of the hotel and stops.

Tony, her driver and trusted bodyguard, makes eye contact with her through the rearview mirror.

"Vickie, you go ahead into the lobby, and I'll take care of the luggage and the check-in."

"You are such a sweetheart," Vickie says to Tony as she steps out of the vehicle. "I'll just wait for you in the lobby. I don't feel like signing autographs right now. I just want to get to the room and order some room service. I'm starving."

No sooner have the words left her mouth than people milling around the entrance of the hotel start yelling, "It's Vickie Shaheen! It's Vickie Shaheen!"

In an instant, she is swarmed by autograph seekers.

Tony immediately jumps out of the limo and takes a position next to her. He starts scanning the crowd with steely eyes. His arms are crossed in front of him. His massive shoulders and cartoon, superhero biceps are clear signals that appropriate decorum on the part of the fans will be strictly enforced.

Accommodating as always to her fans, Vickie is dutifully autographing every piece of paper thrust at her.

She turns her head and catches Tony's eye. He gives her a wink.

It is two days later, and the day of the benefit concert has arrived.

Muscular clouds float lazily across the late-afternoon sun.

Jonathan is maneuvering his carriage into Sarah's driveway. She sits silently next to him, looking straight ahead.

Jonathan pulls back on the reins. The horse clomps to a stop.

He sits back in his seat. After a short pause, he turns towards Sarah. Sarah turns her head away.

"Sarah, I never intended to hurt you. That's why I have always been honest with you."

He places his hand on hers.

Sarah pulls her hand away. "It is very clear to me that you still have strong feelings for the 'English' girl."

"Sarah, I'm not going to lie to you. Yes, I do still have feelings for Vickie."

"Then why are you with me now?"

"I'm here with you because I care about you. But her coming here has stirred up a lot of confusion inside me. I know that's not what you want to hear. But it's the truth."

Sarah turns towards him, her blue eyes flashing. "I'm not confused about my feelings towards you, Jonathan. I want to be more than just a passing fancy to you."

She reaches over and puts her hand on his cheek. "She left you years ago. Her career was more important to her than you were to her. Do you understand that? I will never leave you. I am here now. I will always put you and our family first in my life. And you will never have to choose between me and your own kind, because you and I are cut from the same cloth. And that, Jonathan Schaeffer, is the difference between the two women in your life causing you such confusion."

"I know all this about you. You are everything an Amish man could ever hope for or want. I just don't know if I can ever be the kind of husband you need and deserve. And the fact is, Sarah, I'm not sure you and I are cut from the same cloth."

Sarah pulls her hand away from his face and folds her hands in her lap. "Well, unfortunately for both of us, it is more than likely that you will lose me before you figure things out. In case you've forgotten our ways, we Amish women don't put off marriage and family the way the 'English' do."

"I haven't forgotten," Jonathan replies.

Then, he climbs down from the carriage, walks over to Sarah's side of the carriage, and opens her door.

Without a word, she climbs down from the carriage. He extends a hand to assist her. She ignores it.

He starts to walk with her to her front door.

"I can find my own way, thank you," she says to him coldly.

She walks up the stairs to the front door, opens the door, and without looking back, disappears into the house, closing the door firmly behind her.

Jonathan tips his hat and climbs back into the carriage.

Moments later, he swings the carriage onto the main road.

Sarah is watching from her second-floor bedroom window, hidden behind the blinds.

She reaches up and pulls the cord. The blinds snap shut. She turns away from the window, her face buried in her hands.

CHAPTER VII

The New American Music Theatre sits at the end of a long, circular driveway.

From a distance, the neoclassical building looks like an ancient monument, rising up from the emerald-green countryside.

The theatre has become famous for showcasing an eclectic sampling of talented veteran artists in pop, blues, jazz, and classical music.

From behind the curtain, Vickie is peeking out at the audience, which is bristling with anticipation.

After several minutes of fruitless searching, she turns away in obvious frustration.

Her musicians are already onstage, warming up with their instruments. The dissonant sounds from their instruments clash with her warm-up vocalizing.

Vickie appears particularly nervous tonight. Indeed, this is her first homecoming performance, and it is taking place in front of most of her old friends, many of her relatives, her parents, and presumably, Jonathan.

Her anxiety is obvious to her band leader, Jim, who approaches her. "How are you doing, beautiful?"

She shakes her hands. "Jimmy, I have never been so nervous before a show in my life!"

Jim takes her hands in his. "Look, beautiful, you know how I feel about you being nervous. You're going to blow them out of their seats tonight."

"You think so?"

"I know so. Now take a deep breath, close your eyes, and go through each song in your mind."

"Okay," she says to Jim as she closes her eyes.

Jonathan is dressed in jeans and a sports jacket. The collar on his white shirt is open, and the shirt sleeves poke out fashionably, just beyond the coat sleeves.

He rushes up the stairs to the theater and through the front doorway.

As he approaches the ticket counter, he reaches into his coat pocket for his ticket; nothing there. He stops and tries the other pocket; still nothing. He reaches into all of the pockets of his jeans, one by one; there is no ticket to be found anywhere.

Now, Jonathan finds himself standing in front of the young lady taking tickets at the door, looking helpless and more than a little perplexed. But just like most of the young ladies in town, she knows who Jonathan Schaeffer is.

"What's wrong, Jonathan? Can't find your ticket?" she asks.

"I can't believe it, but yes, I can't find it. I must have left it on top of the dresser. Believe me, I had a ticket."

"You know what? I totally believe you, Jonathan. So don't worry. You go right on in," she says with a dramatic gesture of her hand.

"Thank you so much. You are truly a life saver," he says to her.

He pauses for a moment before grabbing her by the arms and kissing her on the lips.

The young lady reaches for something, anything, to steady herself. "You better hurry, Jonathan. The show is starting in a few minutes," she stammers.

"Thanks again," he says before rushing past her and into the lobby of the theater.

With her cheeks flushing a bright crimson, the young lady straightens her jacket and pats her hair. When she turns around, she lets out a loud, high-pitched gasp. A long line of mostly amused ticket holders has formed in front of her. She mumbles something about how sorry she is and quickly starts grabbing tickets.

Just as soon as Jonathan makes it to the lobby of the theater, it occurs to him that now he has to somehow get by the ushers without a ticket. He looks at his watch. It is 7:58. The show is about to start in a few minutes. He quickly scans the two entry doors on either side of the theater, knowing full well that the job of theater usher tends to attract elderly women with strong authoritarian tendencies. But Jonathan is still on a lucky streak. For whatever reason, the usher at the right entry door is missing in action. Jonathan quickly slips through the doorway.

He walks halfway down the aisle before another realization clangs inside his head. Without a ticket, he has no idea where to sit in the jam-packed theater.

Standing in the aisle, looking lost and hopeless, he makes a three-hundred-and sixty-degree turn.

Just as he turns to walk back up the aisle to the rear of the theater, a hand reaches out and grabs his arm.

He turns around.

Vickie's mother, Veronica, is standing in front of him.

"Mrs. Shaheen?"

"Come with me, Jonathan," she says as she pulls on his arm. Quickly, she leads him down the aisle, all the way to a seat in the front row.

"We have an extra seat that Victoria gave us in case we decided to bring a friend or relative. I guess it was meant for you all along," she explains.

Jonathan kisses her on the cheek. "Mrs. Shaheen, it was a strong wind that blew me down here," he says.

Veronica gives him a hug. "Well, you're here now, and that's all that matters."

Just before Jonathan had taken his seat next to her mother,

Vickie had turned away from behind the curtain. She just missed seeing him. So she still does not know for sure if he is going to be there in the audience.

A chorus line of thoughts starts dancing through her head. "He never called me to confirm that he was coming tonight. But Dad spoke to him and made sure he knew we wanted him to be here. He did tell Dad that he wouldn't want to be any place else tonight. Was he just saying that to not hurt my feelings? I hope he still cares about us. I hope I don't trip and fall on my butt. I hope I don't forget the lyrics. Oh God, I just hope."

"Sixty seconds, everyone, sixty seconds!" the stage manager calls out.

Thankfully, Vickie's brief trip down insanity lane comes to an abrupt end.

Vickie closes her eyes and tries to focus on her opening words to the audience and her first song. In the background, she can hear the show's host introducing her.

"And now, ladies and gentlemen, the moment you have been waiting for, I give you Lancaster's own, international singing star, Vickie Shaheen!"

The audience erupts into a frenzied applause.

The curtain slowly opens, and the backlit silhouette of a woman comes into view at the rear of the stage.

A hush quickly falls over the audience.

Vickie's voice begins to fill the auditorium. She is alone onstage, singing a cappella, and slowly walking towards the audience.

Just as she reaches the front of the stage, the band starts playing.

The spotlights flash on, and the audience gasps.

Jonathan's heart starts doing backflips inside his chest.

Dressed in a neon-yellow skintight dress, Vickie is now standing behind the microphone, her soprano voice soaring above the music.

Blinded by the glare of the spotlights, she cannot see anyone in the audience. She has no idea that Jonathan is sitting in the front row, only a few feet away.

The song is coming to an end now. The band is playing the last few bars. Vickie steps back from the microphone and bows her head.

The audience explodes into a delirium of applause, whistling, and screaming.

Vickie steps up to the microphone. "Thank you, to the people of Lancaster, Pennsylvania, and a special thank you to my family and friends. I want to express my deepest gratitude to all the people who came here tonight to support the Feed the World organization. This cause is very dear to my heart. I have seen, firsthand, the incredible work that they are doing in our country and in countries all over the world. I have personally toured many of the countries where this organization is doing so much good for so many needy people, especially children. This is one organization where most of your donations really end up helping the people who so desperately need your help. And during the intermission and after the show, there will be tables in the lobby where you can get more information about the Feed the World organization, and about how you can further help this worthy cause. Again, thank you for being here tonight, and thank you for all of your support."

The audience applauds politely.

She steps back from the microphone and nods to Jim.

The band starts up again.

The crowd instantly recognizes the song and breaks into a wild applause, even before she starts singing. She bows her head and then steps up to the microphone.

It is intermission now, and Vickie is sitting in her dressing room in front of the mirror, patting her face with a soft towel. She folds the towel neatly, lays it down, and just sits there in her chair, staring at herself in the mirror.

Maggie, her personal assistant, is across the room, arranging her wardrobe for the second set. She looks over at Vickie.

"Honey, you look beautiful. I'll touch up your hair in a minute. I want you to drink water now, lots of water."

"I know. I know. I'm trying. I'm just not a good water-drinker,"

Vickie replies.

"That stuff will keep you young and beautiful," Maggie says to her.

"I finished almost a whole bottle."

"Yes, a whole little bottle. But I suppose that's better than nothing. Now look, I want to pull your hair back for the second set. I want you to look elegant for the ballads. When we make the costume change at the end, we'll let your hair down again. Okay?"

"Sure, Maggie, whatever you want," Vickie answers softly.

Maggie detects a tone in Vickie's voice and walks over to her. "Are you okay, sweetheart?"

"Yes, I'm okay. Why do you ask?"

Maggie starts massaging Vickie's neck and upper back. "You seem a little down right now. You just sang like an angel. The crowd was out of their minds. So what's wrong?"

Vickie closes her eyes. "Nothing's wrong. I'm just conserving energy. I don't want to burn out at the end."

"I can appreciate that, if that were true. Vickie, this is Maggie you're talking to. Now, what's going on? Because this is not about your energy level."

Vickie turns around and faces Maggie. "Maggie, I'm singing for him out there, and I don't even know if he's here."

Maggie squeezes Vickie's shoulders. "Little girl, you've got thousands of people out there, going crazy over you, and all you're worried about is one guy. That is so typical of you artists. The world loves you, but you're not happy unless that one special person loves you. But you know something; the way you are is exactly why you are such an amazing performer. When you sing, people feel the emotion that bubbles up from within you. The music comes alive, and the lyrics really mean something. That's why the world loves you. And if he doesn't see it, and he doesn't hear it, then he doesn't deserve you."

"Thank you, Maggie," Vickie says, patting Maggie's hand. "You are a true friend."

Maggie cradles Vickie's face in her hands. "You better believe that. You know something, you and me; we're going to grow old together."

Vickie hugs Maggie. "I know."

Someone knocks on the dressing room door.

"Oh, come in," Maggie barks.

The stage manager pokes his head through the doorway. "Five minutes, ladies. Shake a leg."

Vickie and Maggie look at each other.

"Five minutes!" Maggie gasps. "Oh we are so unready. Let's go, girl. We've got to get you into this long, black tight little thing in about sixty seconds."

With that said, the two ladies start moving real fast, like two characters in an old, silent movie.

Five minutes later, Vickie is standing in the wings backstage, waiting for the curtains to open.

She is squeezed into a full length strapless black gown. Her hair is pulled back off her face. She is wearing no jewelry, save for a pair of small chandelier diamond earrings, which appear to blink on and off with every movement of her head. As usual, she wears hardly any makeup on her exquisite face, just her usual touch of mascara and bit of lip gloss.

As the curtains begin to open slowly, Vickie looks down and takes a deep breath. When she looks up, she is stunned to discover that she can actually see people sitting out in the audience. Apparently, the seats in the front rows are being illuminated by low-luster ceiling lights located above and in front of the stage.

People are looking around and talking quietly amongst themselves, apparently unimpressed that Vickie is standing up onstage right in front of them. However, it does not take her long to figure out that they are ignoring her because they cannot see her. She is hidden in relative darkness because the high-glare stage spotlights have not yet been turned on.

Just as soon as Vickie realizes that she can see the audience, but they cannot see her, she starts scanning the front rows. In no time at all, she locates Jonathan, sitting in the front row next to her parents. Jonathan has a smile on his face, and he appears to be looking right at her. Her heart flips up into her throat, and her hand comes up to her mouth.

"Oh my God, he's been only a few feet from me the whole time," she whispers to herself.

Her gaze upon Jonathan is short-lived. Seconds after finding him, she loses him again as the stage lights flash on, and he quickly disappears within their blinding glow.

And in an instant, it is Vickie who now materializes onstage in front of the audience, as if she were the pretty lady in a magician's act.

She stands motionless onstage, her hand still covering her mouth.

The audience sits in silence for her moment, no doubt stunned by her sudden appearance in front of them. Then a loud murmuring begins rising up from the audience, and a spattering of clapping quickly becomes a growing crescendo of applause.

She drops her hand from her mouth and starts walking towards the microphone, taking little steps in her tight gown, like a geisha girl. When she reaches the microphone, she makes a half-turn and nods to the band.

Immediately the music begins, and full-throttle applause now bursts from the crowd.

Vickie closes her eyes and bows her head. She slowly lifts her head, and when she begins to sing, a hush quickly falls over the auditorium.

After three encores, Vickie's concert is finally drawing to an end. She is singing the last few lines of a popular torch song.

She lifts the microphone out of the stand and walks over to the edge of the stage, just in front of where Jonathan is sitting. She hitches up her gown just enough to kneel down, near the edge of the stage. She still cannot see him, but now she knows he is there.

Her voice is soaring now; the last high notes so clear and the pitch so perfect, that one can only imagine the voice of an angel. She holds the last high note for what seems like forever, her voice booming through the sound system, and then suddenly, it is over.

The audience sits in silence for a moment, as if in a trance, and then rises en masse in a final standing ovation.

She bows her head and gently lays the microphone on the stage. She slowly lifts her head and looks in Jonathan's direction.

If she could see him, she would know that he is standing and clapping and shaking his head in disbelief.

She stands up and bows low, first in his direction, and then to the audience. Then she steps back from the edge of the stage and waves to the audience.

"Goodnight, everyone. Thank you so much for sharing this evening with us tonight. And remember, drive home carefully."

She turns and raises her hand to acknowledge her band. They bow towards her.

"Thank you, guys. You are the best."

The auditorium lights turn on. There will be no more encores. The show is over.

As the audience again comes into view under the bright, ceiling lights, Vickie turns towards Jonathan, expecting that they will finally be able to acknowledge each other, and all she sees is his empty seat. She quickly looks to her mother for help. All that her mother can do is to give her a perplexed, "I don't know" gesture.

Though deeply upset now, she still manages to keep smiling as she begins walking back towards the band. With her back to the audience, the smile on her face quickly disappears.

The curtain begins to close.

She turns around and waves at the audience one last time before disappearing behind the curtain.

Vickie is sitting slumped on her dressing room chair. Emotionally and physically exhausted, she is slowly wiping off her mascara.

A knock on the door barely gets a rise out of her.

"Yes, come in," she says weakly.

Through the mirror, she sees Jonathan coming through the door.

"Hi," he says as he takes a step towards her.

Vickie jumps up from the chair and turns to face him. She fights the urge to jump into his arms.

"Hello," she replies.

Jonathan takes another step forward. "You were amazing tonight."

"Thank you," she says, as she puts her hands on her hips and narrows her eyes. "I saw you in the front row next to Mom and Dad. I turn around for a lousy second, and when I turn back, you're gone. I thought you left the building."

"I did. But I came back," Jonathan says to her.

"Well, I looked for you, Jonathan. I even went to the lobby looking for you, before coming back here."

Jonathan moves closer. "I'm here now."

"Why did you leave like that? And why are you here now?" Vickie asks, her tone becoming indignant.

"The answer to your first question is because of you. And the answer to the second question is because of you."

"What the hell is that supposed to mean?"

"I left because, after seeing you onstage tonight, I didn't feel that I deserved someone like you. But I came back because I needed to see you and talk to you."

"Well, you saw me onstage," Vickie fires back. "Wasn't that good enough for someone so unworthy as you? And as for talking to me, why not just pick up a bloody phone?"

Jonathan steps to within inches of Vickie. "Victoria, I don't want to argue with you."

Tears begin to well up in her eyes. "Why not? I would love an argument with you right now. An argument with you would be a lot better than nothing at all, which is exactly what I've gotten from you for the last two years."

Jonathan looks down. "I know."

"What do you mean, you know? What is it that you know? Do you know the hell I've been living these last few years, looking out in the audience for you every time I'm onstage, hoping to see you, hoping that you would be waiting for me in my dressing room after every concert? But you were never there, Jonathan. You never came. Until tonight. And then even tonight, you were ready to leave me again!"

Jonathan lunges forward, grabs her by the shoulders, and pulls her close to him.

"You are in my head everyday," he says to her. "I can't stop thinking about you. My only escape from you had been when I would fall asleep at night. Not anymore. Now, you have found your way into my dreams. Now I think about you and dream about you, day and night."

"Well, if you're so hung up on me, you have a funny way of showing it," Vickie answers back. "You know what? Your torment doesn't impress me. What about me? What about my torment? I can't even go out on a date without screwing it up, because I can't stop thinking about my 'farm boy.' Well, I can't do this any more. I don't want to do this anymore. Too many people depend on me. Because of you, I haven't been able to write a new song in months. I'm sick and tired of being miserable all the time."

With that said, Vickie raises her hand as if to slap him.

Jonathan does not flinch. He just keeps looking into her eyes.

She lowers her hand.

He pulls her close and whispers into her ear. "Your torment is my salvation. I know what I want now."

She throws her head back and looks into his eyes, as if searching in them for her next words. But no trenchant words come forth; no dramatic soliloquy.

Instead, her eyes roll back in her head, and she pitches forward, collapsing into his arms.

He lifts her up and carries her over to the dressing room couch.

Just as he is laying her down on the couch, Maggie walks into the dressing room. She looks first at Vickie, lying semi-conscious on the couch, and then at Jonathan, kneeling down next to her.

"What happened?" she cries out as she rushes towards them.

"She's okay, Maggie," he says calmly, without turning. "She just fainted. But she's coming around now. Look, could you get her some water? I think she may be dehydrated."

"Oh, Lord. I knew it. She never drinks enough water during

her concerts. And I don't know when she last ate. I'm always telling her to eat properly and drink more fluids before a concert."

Jonathan puts his hand on Maggie's arm. "Maggie, could you get her some water?"

"Oh, yes, I'll get her some water, right now."

"Thank you, Maggie. That would be good."

Maggie hurries out of the room.

As Jonathan strokes her forehead, Vickie's eyes begin to open slowly. She starts to say something, but Jonathan puts his finger on her lips.

He leans down and kisses her on the forehead. "Don't say anything. Just rest now."

Maggie returns with bottles of orange juice and water.

Vickie turns her head and looks at Maggie through half-closed eyelids.

"How many times have I told you about not drinking enough liquids?" Maggie scolds.

"I know. I know," Vickie replies meekly, her voice weak and raspy. "I've been a bad girl."

Jonathan stands up and steps aside. Maggie sits down on the couch next to Vickie and helps her drink from the water bottle. Vickie then lets her head fall back on the couch pillow and closes her eyes. Maggie turns towards Jonathan. Jonathan gestures that he will call her. Maggie nods okay. Then Jonathan turns and leaves the room.

A moment later, Vickie opens her eyes and grabs Maggie's hand. "Where's Jonathan?" she asks softly, her voice barely audible.

"Don't worry about that right now, honey. You just rest now and keep drinking."

Vickie nods weakly, lifts her head, and takes another sip of water before letting her head fall back again on the pillow.

A few hours later, Jonathan is alone in his studio, sitting at his drafting table. A table lamp is the only light in the room. He is still wearing the same clothes he wore to Vickie's concert earlier that evening. His jacket lies draped over a chair.

With a quiet intensity, Jonathan is putting the finishing

touches on a portrait of Vickie.

Apparently satisfied with the now-completed rendering, Jonathan sits back in his chair and takes a deep breath. He stares at his painting of Vickie's face for a long while, as if expecting that, at any moment, it will come alive and start singing. The painting triggers his memory of the time when he first saw Vickie and heard her sing.

A twelve-year-old Jonathan is steering his horse buggy along the side of a busy main street. He looks up at a banner strung high across the road. The banner reads, "20th Annual Strasburg Music Festival."

This day, Jonathan is not wearing his usual Amish attire. And so it is an "English-looking" Jonathan who swings his very Amish-looking carriage into the parking lot of a large, outdoor amphitheater.

The Strasburg Bowl has long reigned as the town's primary cultural center and the music festival's main venue. The parking lot is packed to the brim.

Jonathan hops out of the buggy and walks over to the ticket booths.

This will be the first time that Jonathan will have attended a live music concert, and the tingling in the back of his neck reflects his excitement. He has known about the music festival for months and decided long ago to attend the event. Now that he is actually here, he can hardly believe it. His emotions are bubbling over as he walks into the open theater.

Minutes before show time, the theater is standing-room only. This suits Jonathan just fine. He finds a place to stand in the back with a good view, just as the announcer begins his introductions.

"We are pleased to welcome to our stage today, performing for the first time in the Strasburg Music Festival, the St. Catherine School's girl choir."

The audience applauds politely, and then quickly quiets down.

The girls, ages ten to fourteen, are standing center stage and wearing white, button-down blouses and dark-blue pleated skirts; the typical parochial school uniform.

The choir conductor taps her baton on the podium. She turns and nods in the direction of the lone musician, a pianist. The accompanist begins playing. The conductor jabs at the air with the baton, and the choir begins singing.

Jonathan closes his eyes and is just starting to lose himself in the pleasing, vocal harmony when he is roused by the sound of a voice soaring above the others. He opens his eyes.

Standing onstage in front of the choir, singing lead vocals, is a twelve-year-old girl. She is as beautiful as her voice.

"Where did she come from?" he asks out loud, to no one in particular.

A woman standing nearby turns to him. "Oh that's Vickie Shaheen. She's well known around here. What a voice she has. Also, she's very pretty, isn't she?"

"Yes, ma'am. She sure is," Jonathan replies, not taking his eyes off the girl onstage.

"Well, you know, you can hear her sing every Sunday at the St. Catherine Church over there in Lancaster. Do you know where that is?" the woman asks with a smile.

"Yes, ma'am, I do. Thank you for the information," Jonathan replies politely.

"You're very welcome."

Jonathan reaches up to tip his hat, but then remembers that today he is not wearing his straw hat.

Vickie finishes her aria and quickly steps back into the front row of the choir. The audience immediately erupts into an ovation. She takes a quick bow. When the applause continues, the girl on her left gently nudges her with an elbow. Vickie finally breaks into a big smile and bows again. When she raises her head, she looks out into the audience.

Jonathan, who is clapping so hard that his palms are getting sore, could swear that she is looking right at him.

Jonathan could swear that the painting of Vickie is looking

right at him.

He stands up and walks over to where his coat lays draped over the chair. He reaches into the inside pocket of the jacket and pulls out an envelope. He walks slowly back to his chair and collapses into it, finally looking exhausted from the long day.

He looks at the envelope, taps it on the table and then looks at it again. He raises the envelope to the light, examines it for a moment, and then taps it on the table again.

The envelope is addressed to: "Mr. Jonathan Schaeffer."

The return address is: "The New York School of Fine Arts, Office of Admissions."

Sitting slumped in his chair, he starts tapping the envelope on his forehead. A few moments pass by, and then suddenly, he sits straight up in his chair.

"Enough!" he yells out.

He takes a deep breath and tears open the envelope. He snatches out the single-page letter and reads it quickly, his eyes darting back and forth. A big smile cracks his dour expression. He leaps out of the chair and stabs his fist into the air. "Yes!"

CHAPTER VIII

One month later, it is eleven o'clock p.m. in New York City, and Times Square is ablaze in lights.
In the center of this kaleidoscope of lights, colors, and sounds is a giant billboard, hanging high on the side of a skyscraper. In the center of the billboard is a painting of Vickie's face. This rendering of Vickie's face is a huge blow-up of Jonathan's painting, the very same one he created the night of the Feed the World concert in Lancaster, Pennsylvania one month ago.
The billboard is advertising Vickie's concert this evening at Madison Square Garden.

The sold-out concert has just ended, and thousands of fans are now streaming out of the Garden. While many people are jumping into waiting taxis, most are walking down Seventh Avenue and Thirty-First and Thirty-Second Streets.

Vickie is in her dressing room. Not one to hang around after a performance, she has already changed into her civilian clothes and is now putting on an overcoat.
Vickie is feeling very satisfied. Always her own toughest critic, she knows that she performed well tonight. The concert was a

smashing success. The audience gave her one standing ovation after another. And on top of that, her newly released album is flying off the racks at the record stores. But in spite of all this success, Vickie still cannot shake the melancholy that grips her day and night.

Maggie enters the dressing room. "Honey, how are you getting home tonight?"

Vickie turns towards her. "What do you mean, how am I getting home tonight?"

"There's no limo outside," Maggie answers, matter-of-factly.

"What do you mean...there's no limo outside?"

"Honey, do you want me to draw you a picture?"

"Oh, that's cute, Maggie. I'll just ride home on the picture of the limo. How about that? Maggie, you're supposed to know these things."

"Now, young lady, if I knew what was going on, wouldn't I tell you?" Maggie replies, feigning indignation, her hands on her hips.

"I'm sorry, Maggie. I'm not blaming you. It's just that I'm worried. Do you think something happened to Tony? Where do you think he is? I'm going to call him right now."

She pulls her cell phone out of her coat pocket and speed-dials his number. The call transfers to Tony's voice mail. Vickie looks at Maggie. "Now I'm really worried, Maggie. I hope he's okay."

Maggie looks at Vickie for a moment and then grabs her by the shoulders. "Vickie, let's go outside and see if Tony is waiting there right now. Maybe he's standing outside the car and just left his phone inside the car. I do that all the time."

Vickie quickly agrees. "Okay, if that's what you think we should do. If anything's happened to that big lug, I don't know what I would do."

Maggie takes Vickie's arm, and they quickly walk out of the dressing room and start heading down a backstage hallway.

As they walk down the dim corridor, Maggie turns to Vickie. "Did I tell you how amazing you were tonight? And that crowd... they just loved you."

"Thanks, Maggie. I know you're trying to take my mind off

things, but I can't really think about any of that right now."

"I know, honey."

Maggie pushes through a heavy, metal door, and they walk outside into the cold, midnight air. Vickie stops Maggie with a gentle tug on her arm. They both look around. No Tony. And no limousine. Vickie walks a bit further away from the building and looks down the street, both ways. Nothing.

After a performance, Vickie is accustomed to being escorted from buildings by burly security guards and rushed into waiting limousines, which then quickly speed away. Tonight, she finds herself in the very unfamiliar and uncomfortable position of standing outside a side exit of Madison Square Garden at midnight, with no transportation, and with only Maggie as her security detail. And to make matters worse, they are in the middle of a block where taxis are speeding past them on their way to where the real business is located, just around the corner on Seventh Avenue, where the sidewalks are teeming with thousands of potential fares.

Just as a sense of vulnerability is starting to creep into Vickie's consciousness, giving her a sick feeling in her gut, she turns and sees a horse and carriage sitting at the curb directly in front of her.

A man is sitting in the driver's seat. He is wearing a hat pulled down low over his eyes, a wool scarf around his neck, and a heavy coat, buttoned all the way to the top.

He turns towards Vickie. "Ma'am, would you like a ride somewhere?"

Now looking even more perplexed, Vickie turns to Maggie. "What in the world is a horse and buggy doing here?"

Maggie shrugs. "I don't know. Maybe it's something new for the tourists in the area."

The two women stand together in silence for a few moments, staring at the horse and buggy. Vickie is standing there, holding the collar of her coat tightly around her neck, when she starts to sense a growing feeling of comfort in seeing the horse carriage with its driver sitting there just a few yards away.

Maggie suddenly grabs Vickie's arm. "Vickie, I've got an idea," she says excitedly. "Why don't you have him take you around to Seventh Avenue where you can then catch a cab? It's a good way to get to where the cabbies are. And the carriage will be a perfect cover for you from the fans. No one would expect you to be in a horse carriage at this time of night, in this part of town."

Vickie looks at her as if she thinks Maggie has lost her mind. Crazy or not, Maggie presses on. "I would go with you, but I really should stay back and look out for Tony. If he shows up, I can ring you on the cell phone, and we'll come and pick you up. It's a good plan. You know you can't just wait here. It's not safe. And you can't walk around to Seventh. The area is too crowded with fans. Right now, as strange as it seems, the carriage is your best option."

Vickie sighs and shakes her head. "This is a shame when my best option is a horse and buggy in the middle of Manhattan. All right, okay. Let's do this before I change my mind."

Maggie leads Vickie over to the carriage. "Excuse me, sir, she would like a ride to Seventh Avenue," Maggie says, looking up at the driver.

The driver nods his head and climbs down from the carriage. Then he opens the carriage door and extends his hand. "Ma'am."

Vickie walks over, takes his hand, and climbs up into the carriage.

"Thank you," she murmurs softly.

"You're welcome," he answers in a low, hoarse voice.

Vickie wrinkles her nose. "Are you taking something for that cold of yours?" she asks the man.

"Yes, ma'am, I am."

"I sure hope so. And please be careful of the cars."

"Don't worry, ma'am. I've been doing this sort of thing my whole life," he replies as he climbs up into the driver's seat. He releases the parking brake, gives the horse a tap on its hindquarters, and off they go, the horse hugging the curb as the carriage makes its way towards Seventh Avenue.

Maggie smiles sweetly at Vickie and waves. Vickie frowns back at her.

Maggie watches them for a few moments as they pull away, and then turns to walk back towards the building. As she approaches the exit door at the side of the building, she gives a thumbs-up sign to a big lug of a guy standing in the shadows.

As the carriage moves slowly towards Seventh Avenue, Vickie is overtaken by a profound fatigue. She rests her head against the back of the seat, closes her eyes, and quickly dozes off.

When she opens her eyes again, they have already arrived at the curbside in front of the Seventh Avenue entrance to Madison Square Garden.

Startled, Vickie quickly sits up in her seat. "I must have fallen asleep," she says out loud.

"It's not like riding on the back of a galloping horse back home on the farm, is it, ma'am?" the driver asks without turning around, in a deep voice, not at all hoarse or raspy.

Vickie's eyes brighten. "You're right about that. Those were great times. And I really miss…"

She stops mid-sentence, leans forward in her seat, and now looks—really looks—at the driver for the first time.

"How would you know about my riding on the back of a horse?" she asks in a huffy tone.

Without answering the question, the driver pulls his hat even lower over his eyes, climbs down from his seat, and steps over to Vickie's side of the carriage. He opens the carriage door and offers her his hand.

With her eyes fixed on the carriage driver, she takes his hand and steps down from the carriage and onto the sidewalk.

A large crowd is still milling around the front entrance of the Garden, and Vickie is quickly being recognized by a rapidly growing number of concertgoers. But because her eyes remain glued to the driver, she is oblivious to the bristling crowd closing in on her.

Still holding her hand, the carriage driver removes his hat and looks straight into her eyes.

The city lights illuminate his face.

"Jonathan!" Vickie gasps.

Jonathan raises her hand to his lips and kisses it. "This ride is on the house, Miss Shaheen."

Without another word, she leaps into his arms.

And he spins her around to the cheering and clapping of the circling crowd.

THE END

About the Author

R P Gabriel lives in Connecticut with his beautiful wife and four children. He is a graduate of the University of California, at Berkeley.

Made in the USA
Lexington, KY
18 January 2010